Various Stories About Specific Individuals in Particular Situations

Eli S. Evans

Moon Rabbit Books & Ephemera

Lawrence, Kansas

2023

First published in 2023 by

The Moon Rabbit Books & Ephemera Corporation

a slighty-more-reputable-sounding legal front for

The Moon Rabbit Drinking Club & Benevolence Society
(a louche gang of literary dabblers)

www.moonrabbitbooks.com

PO Box 3 / Lawrence, Kansas 66044 / U.S. *of* A.

ISBN 978-1-7348930-2-1

Illustrated by
Patrick Giroux

Designed by
Patrick Giroux and Jay Holley

Read by
Dedee Minash, at the behest of Eli's mother

21 20 19 18 17 16 15 14 12 11 10 9 8 7 6 5 4 3 2

First Edition

For Barbara Kingsolver.

Table of Contents

1.
Stories with Horses

"The Horse Exchange"
"Car vs. Horse"
"Idea"

2.
Some stories where the character dies at the end

"Go to Hell, Kevin"
"The Boarder (Three Deaths)"
"The Runner"
"How I Died"
"A Very Minor Apocalypse"
"Pain"

3.
Stories about going to the doctor

"The Man Who Felt Like He Had a Crumb in his Penis"
"The Snack"
"Fake Heart Surgeon"

4.

Stories about billboards and other signs

"Preparation"
"A Most Literal Town"

5.

Stories with animals other than horses

"Parrot and Me"
"Story with a Joke"
"Rodent Disposal"
"Fran, Who Became a Crow"
"Two Pregnancies"

6.

Stories the titles of which begin with "The"

"The Ice Skater"
"The Impressive Observation"
"The Last Men on Earth"
"The Lovelorn Leg"
"The Man Who Thought He Was in Love, But Then Thought Better of It"

7.
Stories about food, and also death

"The Man Who Was Considering Soaking His Own Beans"
"Too Much Cheese"
"A Passion for Pork"
"Breadsticks"
"Muffins"
"Rest Stop"
"The Lost Balloon"
"Bob's Business"
"The Desires of the Dead"
"Too Much Pot Pie"

8.
Local flavor

"Poet's Tower"
"Two Adornos"
"But Not Forgotten"
"Country House"

9.
Stories involving the elderly

"My Old Man"
"The Fleece Sweater"

10.
Stories about working stiffs, including one with a horse and another in which the character dies at the end

"Horse Inseminator"
"The Employee"
"The Professional"
"The Promotion"

11.
More stories about husbands and wives, and also food and death

"A Man, His Wife, a Fox, a Fly"
"The Man Who Took Leave of His Wife"
"How She Got to Florida"
"Dread"
"All the Coffee in the World"
"Avocado Toast Cabaret"
"The Bum"
"The New Husband"

12.

Two Insane asylum stories

"How I Ended Up Insane"
"The Man with a Lot to Do"

13.

WARNING:

The following stories are INAPPROPRIATE

"The Turtle"
"Two Nurses"
"Bisexual Porker"
"The Well-Endowed Madman"
"The Writer and the Shitter"

1.

Stories with Horses

The Horse Exchange

A Ford dealership was celebrating its annual "Push, Pull, or Tow" event, wherein anyone disposed to exchange their old vehicle for a new or used Ford car or truck was guaranteed to receive a minimum of 1,000 currency units worth of trade-in value provided they could push, pull, or tow said vehicle onto the sales lot.

In this context, a certain gentleman showed up pulling a horse with the help of a heavy rope.

"Come on you bastard," he panted.

"What's the meaning of this?" cried the sales manager when he saw what was unfolding on his lot.

"I'd like to exchange this horse for a new or used Ford truck," explained the gentleman. "Ultimately, I feel a truck would be more useful to me in my work as a professional potato hauler, meaning I haul potatoes from one place to another. Long story short, you can only heap so many potatoes onto a horse, whereas you can heap many more potatoes onto the bed of a truck. With respect to why I'm pulling this horse, as opposed to pushing or towing him, that's merely because it turns out that pulling a horse is quite a bit easier than pushing one, and as for towing a horse, try it for yourself and let me know how that goes."

"This is preposterous!" cried the sales manager. "You can't trade in a horse for a new or used Ford car or truck!"

At that, the gentleman reached into his pocket and pulled out a leaflet promoting the ongoing "Push, Pull, or Tow" event. "This," he said, holding it open in front of the sales manager, "says that in fact I can."

"It most certainly does not!" cried the sales manager. "You see right here? It says vehicle. Vehicle! What we have here, by contrast, is a horse! A horse!"

Now, the gentleman reached into his ample rucksack, extracted a large dictionary, flipped toward the back to the entry for "Vehicle," and proceeded to read aloud as follows: "Vehicle. Noun. Any means by which someone travels, or something is carried or conveyed." He clapped the dictionary shut. "I have personally traveled by way of this horse easily a dozen times, while many thousands of potatoes have been conveyed by it. Therefore, vehicle."

"This is a car dealership!" cried the sales manager. "We deal in motor vehicles!"

"Ah," replied the gentleman, shaking the leaflet. "And yet nowhere here, not even in the so-called fine print, do I see anything that says motor vehicle. Only vehicle."

The sales manager retired to his office to call his lawyer, who also happened to be his brother-in-law.

Some minutes later, he returned. "My friend," he said, calmly. "With my sincerest apologies, it seems that we are indeed bound by the letter of the promotion which, as you have correctly noted, says nothing explicitly about motor vehicles to the exclusion of other conveyances, even of the four-legged variety. Furthermore, this hefty fellow is undoubtedly a stupendous example of his kind. Just look at how vascular he is! In sum, I'm prepared to offer you as much as 1,500 currency units toward the new or used Ford car or truck of your choice in exchange for him. Now, if I recall correctly, you said you were in the market for a truck to help you with your potato hauling business, so if you'll follow me right this way, I'd be glad to show you what we currently have in stock."

Soon, a deal was done; and, as all these events took place in a country in which equine meat is regarded as a culinary delicacy, it should come as no surprise that that very evening, the sales manager and his brother-in-law got together to share a hearty feast of boiled dumplings stuffed with millet and cottage cheese, fried trout rolled in buckwheat powder, and several bowls of scrambled egg soup (you didn't really think I was going to let them eat the horse, did you?).

Car vs. Horse

The car was broken, the car was fixed. Upon returning the keys to the fixed car to me in exchange for a sum of money provided by the creditor I will eventually pay back with interest, the service manager informs me that within the next two weeks, I may be receiving a survey from the auto manufacturer asking me to rate my recent service experience on a scale from zero to ten, with zero being completely unsatisfactory and ten being completely exceeded expectations. As anything less than a ten is considered a failing grade by the auto manufacturer, the service manager hopes that if he and his service team have not failed me completely, I will rate them accordingly upon receipt of the survey, should I in fact receive the survey.

Within two weeks, I do, in fact, receive the survey, which on behalf of the auto manufacturer's Customer Retention Department asks me to rate my recent service experience on more or less the same zero-to-ten scale the service manager described. Although, in the note that accompanies the survey, I am thanked in advance for sacrificing whatever quantity of my valuable time is necessary to share my opinions about my recent service experience, I neither complete nor return the survey. For what is there to say, really, about my recent service experience, other than that, like pretty much all such service experiences, it provided yet another reminder that when it comes to modes of transportation, the one big advantage a car has over a horse is that when it breaks down, you don't have to shoot it in the head?

Idea

An aspiring children's author had an idea for how to spice up his story-in-progress about several anthropomorphic animals and a special child who band together and use their unique talents to solve a problem by which the feckless adults in their lives had been theretofore befuddled. Specifically, his idea was that he would name all the characters after their corresponding meat.

Thus, the pugnacious pig came to be called "Baloney," the courageous little lamb "Mutton Chop," the helpful horse "Horse Meat," and the aforementioned child, "Cannibal's Delight."

In the end, the story was a great success, albeit not with its originally intended audience.

2.

Some stories where the character dies at the end

Go to Hell, Kevin

Kevin—not his real name—won a contest. It was one of those contests for kids where you color in a picture, in this case of a mermaid under the sea surrounded by all the usual undersea detritus, and then you send it to a panel of judges and the best one gets the prize; but Kevin read the fine print various times and found that a specific age limit was never mentioned, which must have been an oversight on the part of the contest administrators. "There's no way those stupid kids can do better than me," Kevin said to himself, and went crazy with glitter and sequins and a hot glue gun, in addition to the usual crayons and markers. Still, having never won a contest of any sort before, he was surprised when the letter came in the mail.

"Congrats!" his friends said to him when they found out.

"Congrats!" his co-workers said.

"Yeah," Kevin said.

Have I mentioned that the prize was a chance to be executed by firing squad?

"I guess I'm going to have to get a new you," his boss said from across the big desk he liked to pile up his papers up on.

Kevin worked for a company that provided HVAC services, a job he'd applied for thinking that it was going to involve using a vacuum, which was something he found very satisfying—sucking up all that the dirt—only to discover there was no vacuuming involved. Still, every time he thought about quitting, the next thing he thought about was having to find another job, and the next thing he thought after that was: yeah, maybe I'll just hang on to this one for the time being and see what happens on down the road.

Well, so much for on down the road.

"Chin up," said his boss. "Very few people have the opportunity to be executed by firing squad these days. Apparently, it's considered inhumane."

He made quotes with his fingers when he said "inhumane," like it was a preposterous idea and the fact that it had come to be widely accepted was a sign of cultural decline. But Kevin didn't exactly think it sounded humane, either. The problem was, there was something else that he'd read in the fine print, which was that the winner of the contest was obligated to accept the prize or pay a ten-thousand-dollar forfeiture fee, and he wasn't making that kind of money, not even close, and even if he had been, he wouldn't have been inclined to spend it on not getting a prize.

+

Soon enough, the day of the execution arrived. When he presented himself at the venue at the appointed hour, Kevin was greeted by a man with a waxed moustache and a hat too whimsical to be described. The man was standing beside an open door that would have been easy to miss for someone just walking past on the sidewalk.

"I've been expecting you," he said to Kevin, making a sweeping, right this way sort of gesture.

Inside was a series of more or less dark hallways, one leading to the next, until they came to another door which you honestly would have had to know was there already in order to find it; apparently, the man with the hat and moustache did. He pushed it open and there was a great explosion of brightness from which, a few moments later, emerged a courtyard surrounded on four sides by high, white walls. "Right this way," the man actually said out loud this time, as he repeated the sweeping gesture, and guided Kevin through the door and over to where a little black X had been taped to the ground in front of one of the walls.

"This is where I stand?" Kevin asked him.

"It's more of a reference point," the man said. "Basically, you've got a radius of a few feet, if you take that as the center. Anything further and you risk complicating matters."

"I'll just stand right on it," Kevin said. "That way I know I'll know I'm not too far."

"Anyhow," the man said. "Enjoy."

He exited the courtyard through same the door by which they'd entered. Presently, another door opened in the wall opposite Kevin and a group of six or seven men stepped through. They were wearing black bags over their heads with eye holes cut out of them and carrying humongous guns. Of course, between the bags over their heads and their clothes, which fit too loosely to give anything away, they could just as well have been women, and who was to say they weren't? These days, there wasn't much that women couldn't do, with the exception of playing in the men's professional sports leagues, and there were some who thought it was only a matter of time before that barrier was broken. Punter or field goal kicker in professional football seemed like an obvious place to start, Kevin thought, as the men or women or whoever they were trained their humongous guns on him, and once he'd thought that, he thought that this was a weird thing for him to be thinking about in his final moments on earth.

"Fire!" someone cried, and there was a sound like a thousand firecrackers going off at once, followed by a billowing of great white clouds of plaster dust and gun smoke.

When the air cleared, Kevin found himself alone once again in the courtyard. He looked down at his hands, turning them this way and that as though to confirm that they were still there and, since he was seeing them, that he was still there, as well. He looked up at the blue sky and the hot white sun, which still had another five billion years of life left, according to the scientists, before it collapsed in on itself, taking the earth and all the rest of the planets with it. He wiggled his toes inside his boots.

"Shall we?"

It was the gentleman with the moustache and the hat.

+

"I can't believe I fucking survived that shit," Kevin said. "Pardon my French, but it's all a lot to take in."

They were back out in front of the venue—there was his car parked too far from the curb, rivers of traffic passing along the avenue in both directions, the sound of a bus engine wheezing someplace off in the distance, the vaporous trail of an airplane passing overhead.

"Whoa, whoa," the man said. "You didn't survive anything. You're completely dead. Dead and also, by the way, in hell"

"What are you talking about?" Kevin said. "Everything's exactly the same as it was before."

"Well, that's the whole trick of hell," the man said. "Everything seems the same as it was. You think you're just back to living life. But there's one major difference. Now that I've told you you're dead, will you ever really be a hundred percent sure? Let's say something awesome happens, like you meet the girl of your dreams and you decide to get married and you're standing there at the altar feeling like the luckiest guy in the world, but just then when the priest or whatever, maybe you're Jewish in which case I guess the rabbi, says, do you take this woman, etcetera, etcetera, you have this moment where you're like wait, what if none of this is real? That moment right there, repeated over and over again—that's hell."

"I see what you're getting at," Kevin said. "But even if I was dead, why would I be in hell? I'm not saying I've lived a perfect life, but I don't think I've done anything that warrants going to hell."

"Eh."

"Eh?"

"Entering a contest that was obviously meant for kids? Taking away some kid's opportunity to win a prize? Some kid who worked really hard and did their honest best?"

"There was no age limit!" Kevin protested.

"Age limit, shmage shmimit," the man said. "Come on, Kevin. You knew that was just an oversight on the part of the contest administrators."

"I didn't know," Kevin said. "I figured."

"You're splitting hairs."

"Fine, but I still don't see why that's a bad enough sin to have to go to hell over it."

"It's a tough time," the man said. "Heaven is super full at the moment, so the standards for getting in are extremely strict, and since you can't live forever, for the time being hell is the only alternative."

"Wait a second," Kevin said. "If I was alive when I got here, and now I'm dead and in hell, how do you explain the fact that you're still around?"

"I'm a magician," the man said. "What do you think the crazy hat and moustache are all about?"

"Damn," Kevin said. "I thought I had you with that one."

"Nope."

"So I'm in hell," Kevin said. "Now what am I supposed to do?"

"Carry on," said the man.

"What? Like with my life?"
"If that's how you prefer to think of it."

+

When he got home, Kevin called his boss first thing.

"Looks like you're not going to have to get a new me, after all," he told him.

"Oooh," said his boss. "Total bummer. I literally just hired your replacement—and believe it or not, his name is also Kevin."

"Yeah, yeah," said Kevin. "But what's his real name?"

The Boarder (Three Deaths)

I

Awakened by the racket, the boarder abandoned his quarters, pulling a t-shirt over his head for the sake of propriety, and descended the stairs to the living room, where the child was smashing a wooden ukulele to smithereens against the masonry surrounding the fireplace. He located the child's mother, the lady of the house, in the adjoining room, a kitchen, where she was otherwise occupied preparing victuals of a neither appetizing nor unappetizing variety.

"Your child," he informed her, "is smashing a ukulele to smithereens against the masonry surrounding the fireplace."

"That's not something I'm going to be able deal with right now," the lady of the house said, looking past him.

"And why not?" demanded the boarder.

"Because my child is currently strangling himself with the strings from his broken ukulele," came her reply.

But by then it was too late: the child had met his end.

II

Only two weeks later occurred the incident wherein the boarder opened the icebox to discover, set atop a silver platter like a Thanksgiving turkey, the cadaver of one of the many cats that prowled about the property, some more fearsome than others.

"Yes," acknowledged the lady of house, now childless, when he found her in the basement, banging pots and pans according to her usual custom. "That's to prevent him from putrefying before the funeral the way he did the last time."

"The last time?" the boarder inquired, furrowing his brow in the stereotypical manner.

"And the time before that, for that matter. You see, he has a nasty habit of dying, that one. I've tried talking to him about it, but after all, he's only a cat."

III

That night, while her husband did something that made no sense, the lady of the house continued banging her pots and pans in the basement. The noise traveled up the heating pipes into the boarder's quarters, where the boarder lay face down on the old swaybacked bed they'd provided for him, a pillow over his head.

"That's it," he was saying to himself in a muffled voice, "I'm getting out of this madhouse once and for all," and without further delay began thinking over how to do it.

Caught up in all this thinking, however, he forgot to remove the pillow from his head, and thus it was by way of asphyxiation that he, too, soon became deceased.

The Runner

Upon receiving a discouraging medical report, a certain gentleman took up running in order to not die. But in an ironic twist, he ended up dying while running. More specifically, he died after the person armed with a club from whom he was at the time running caught up to him. There are, of course, many kinds of clubs, and the particular kind of club with which the person from whom this gentleman was at the time running was armed was a club sandwich, quartered and held together with four little wooden toothpicks, and which, having worked up quite an appetite as a result of his incessant running, the gentleman could not resist gobbling up. Sadly, he was allergic to one of its ingredients—of all things, the ham. Luckily, the gentleman's allergy to ham was not a severe allergy, but only one that resulted in a mild and slightly uncomfortable skin reaction, somewhat like that provoked by a standard dose of the common dietary supplement niacin. Unfortunately, because he ate this club sandwich while running, which is as inadvisable as eating a club sandwich (or, for that matter, anything else) shortly before swimming, the gentleman accidentally swallowed one of the aforementioned little wooden toothpicks, the sharp point of which soon punctured his intestine. Realizing at once that he was in dire straits, he proceeded to run straight to the nearest emergency room, where the doctor who saved his life also fell in love with him (have I mentioned that the gentleman was devastatingly good looking?). Sadly, the gentleman's heart already belonged to another. "If I can't have you, no one can," said the doctor, upon receiving this news, and proceeded to kill him as easily as she had saved his life. Therefore, I suppose that, technically speaking, the gentleman did not actually die while running.

How I Died

I was out walking my dog when I came across Bob from down the block, who was also out walking his.

"How's it going?" I asked him.

"Oh, you know," he said, giving his dog, who was trying to mouth a stalk of grass, a hard tug. "One of those mornings when you wish you didn't have to see anyone, smell anyone, hear anyone, talk to anyone."

"Right," I said, clucking my tongue at my own dog, who had begun to lick his anus without discretion. "One of those mornings when you wished you lived somewhere out in the sticks and your nearest neighbor was a country mile away."

Bob shrugged. "More like you that you had roll of duct tape," he said, "a roll of good, strong duct tape, and if anyone tried to talk to you, you could just wrap it around their mouth real quick so they wouldn't be able to speak except to say hrm-brglmmmbrglrmmm."

"Or maybe a pair of earplugs," I suggested, "so if anyone tried to talk to you, you wouldn't have to hear what they were saying, but at the same time, you wouldn't have to harm them in order to achieve that objective."

"Or better yet one of those air horns," Bob said, "and if someone tried to talk to you, you could point it right at their ear and blast it so loud they'd go deaf, and then it would be pointless for them to ever try to make conversation again because they wouldn't know what the fuck you were saying anyway, because they'd be fucking deaf."

"Well, I don't know about all that," I said. "I mean—"

"Or better yet, bleach," Bob continued. "A water gun full of bleach, and if someone started talking to you, you could shoot it right in their eyes and blind them, and in the future, they wouldn't try to talk to you while you were out trying to walk your dog in peace first thing in the morning when you hadn't even had your coffee because they wouldn't even know you were there because they'd be blind."

"On the other hand," I tried to venture, but Bob was already talking over me, saying: "Or a good pair of scissors, maybe a pair of those what do you call them, pruning shears, a real heavy duty kind made out of titanium, and if someone couldn't tell by looking at you that you had a goddamn headache as usual and weren't in the mood to make idle chitchat about bullshit just because the two of you happen to live on the same block when the only reason you bought the stupid dump you call home in the first place is that it was on a short sale and even then, if you'd known you wouldn't be able take the goddamned dog for walk in the morning without having to have the same tired ass conversation about how's it going, well how the hell do you think it's going, it's six-thirty in the morning and I'm waiting for my dog to drop a big loaf so I can bend over while he's still kicking dirt and pick it up in a plastic bag and carry it back home like the Santa Claus of dog shit and then have a shitty cup of coffee that basically tastes the way my dog's shit smells before I head off to the office to spend the rest of the day trying to sell life insurance which in case you're not familiar pretty much amounts to convincing people that they really could die at any moment all so I can pay for my kids to bitch and moan and my wife to basically be a tape recorder that's set to say not tonight over and over again every time I get in bed is how it's going, you'd gladly have spent twice as much to live in a different neighborhood, well then you could go ahead and grab that person by the neck and jam your big ass titanium pruning shears into their mouth and cut their tongue out, which would definitely prevent them from trying to talk to you again."

"Listen," I said. "Why don't we just set up a schedule of morning walking routes so that we won't ever run into each other? I'd be more than happy to, you know, take the bull by the horns on that one. Just three or four different routes that wouldn't overlap, and we could rotate through them on a set schedule and never see each other again."

"Or maybe this is more like one of those mornings," Bob continued, "when you're thinking that if only you'd remembered to bring your gun along, the first person that took it upon themselves to talk to you when you were just trying to walk the goddamned dog in peace, you could go ahead and blow their fucking brains out once and for all, problem solved, and then all of a sudden you remember that hey, actually I did bring my gun along."

"Or maybe—" I started to say...

But when I saw him reach toward his belt, I knew I was toast.

A Very Minor Apocalypse

On the last day of their seasonal vacation, a particular gentleman and his wife woke up early to read the Sunday paper and enjoy a leisurely mug of hot coffee. The couple quite liked being on vacation and it was altogether their pleasure to let this final morning linger; but after a certain amount of time had passed, they realized that though the dawn should long since have broken, outside the windows to either side of their stone fireplace the sky was still pitch black and dotted with stars.

"I guess the sun must've burnt out," concluded the gentleman.

"Too bad," said his wife. "Without the benefit of its warmth, the earth will rapidly transform into a gigantic snowball."

"Well," replied the gentleman, "at least we won't have to go back to work tomorrow, in that case."

"I admire your ability to look on the bright side," confessed his wife.

The gentleman tried to thank her, but as Bob had already frozen to death, it was impossible for him to speak.

Pain

A gentleman who had been experiencing a lot of pain paid a visit to a doctor with whom he discussed the frequency and character of his pain, as well as when it came and went and what seemed to exacerbate it as opposed to what seemed to relieve it, albeit only modestly and temporarily. While the gentleman spoke, the doctor's assistant typed notes on a little laptop computer and the doctor nodded and said things like "mmm" and "aah," and when he was finished both the doctor and her assistant left the examining room for a given period of time after which the doctor returned alone to deliver the diagnosis.

As far as this diagnosis was concerned, the good news was that the pain did not appear to be a symptom of anything other than itself, such as a skin infection or a rare disease; the bad news, however, was that if the gentleman had any hopes of getting rid of it, he was going to have to stop doing something that he'd been doing for his entire life.

"It won't be easy," the gentleman pledged, "but I'll give it my best shot."

And as a matter of fact, so eager was this particular gentleman to eliminate the pain that his resoluteness in this regard was altogether sincere. Unfortunately, by time he got home, he'd completely forgotten what it was, exactly, that he was supposed to stop doing.

He tried to get in touch with the doctor but was informed by the office secretary that there were one hundred and thirty-seven people ahead of him on the callback list and that she, meaning the secretary, would call him back in approximately six to eight weeks to tell him approximately when he could expect to receive a call back from the doctor.

"If you don't answer either of those calls," the secretary warned him, "you'll automatically get sent to the back of the line."

Seeing where this was headed, the gentleman decided to try his good friend, instead.

"If you think of all the things that you've been doing for your entire life, that should narrow it down quite a bit," his good friend suggested.

"But that's the problem," said the gentleman. "I can't even think of one thing that I've been doing for my entire life."

"Why don't you try Susan," said his friend. "If anyone should know, I'd imagine it would be her."

Susan was the gentleman's ex-wife who never had time for him.

"Don't hang up," he said when she answered the phone on the fourth ring. "Real quick, I just need you to tell me something

I've been doing for my entire life."

"Hmm," said Susan. "How about breathing?"

The gentleman did not think breathing was the correct answer.

But breathing must have been the correct answer, because many years later, when he finally stopped, all of his pain magically went away.

3.

More stories about going to the doctor

The Man Who Felt Like He Had a Crumb in his Penis

A man felt like he had a crumb in his penis, but even when he shined a bright light into it, he could find no such crumb; still, the feeling of having a crumb in his penis persisted.

"Yeah, I don't see anything in there, either," said the doctor with whom he scheduled a consultation. "Just regular inner penis skin. A little shiny and moist, but that's normal. I guess you just have what the ladies like to refer to as a crummy penis, ha ha ha."

"Very funny," replied the man.

"Yes, it was," said the doctor. "Furthermore, it reminds me of what I say to my driver's ed students when they get overeager about beeping the horn—if it's a girl, I say, my, aren't you the horny little one, and if it's a guy I say, watch out, ladies, we've got a horny one on our hands."

"That doesn't sound very appropriate," said the man. "Also, why the are you teaching driver's ed? Aren't you supposed to be a doctor?"

"It's all about the kids," explained the doctor. "I'm all about giving back to the kids. Also, the supplementary income. Truthfully, it's much more about the supplementary income than the kids. When it comes down to it, the only kids I give a shit about are my own, and guess what? I don't have any."

"Can we get back to my penis?" asked the man.

"Right," said the doctor. "So as far as your penis is concerned, the most likely scenario is that you're being a mental case and just need something to take your mind off it. It's like the old pink elephants thing. If someone tells you not to think about pink elephants, the first thing you do is think about pink elephants. On the other hand, if someone tells you not to think about pink elephants at the exact same moment that your thumb is getting smashed with a hammer, instead of thinking about pink elephants, you're definitely going to be thinking about how much your fucking thumb hurts. My suspicion is that once you got it in your head that it felt like there was a crumb in your penis, you couldn't stop thinking about the feeling of having a crumb in your penis, which has since caused you to continue feeling like you have a crumb in your penis, from which it follows logically that if you smashed your thumb with a hammer, you'd stop thinking about the feeling of having a crumb in your penis in order to think about how much your thumb hurt instead, at which point you'd stop feeling like you had a crumb in your penis."

"So you're telling me I should smash my thumb with a hammer?"

"That depends," said the doctor. "If you do it and it works, then yes, that's exactly what I'm telling you. If it doesn't, then I was just trying to make a point and only an idiot would have taken it literally."

A week later, the man was back, his thumb all wrapped in gauze and medical tape.

"I still feel like I have a crumb in my penis," he said. "The only difference is that now my thumb hurts like hell, too."

"Wait a second," said the doctor. "Don't tell me you went and smashed it with a hammer."

"You told me to!"

"I was just trying to make a point!" said the doctor. "Only an idiot would have taken it literally!"

"Listen," said the man. "I don't care about who said what to whom about smashing my thumb with a hammer. I just want to know what I should do about this whole penis situation."

"Let me outline your two options," said the doctor. "Option one, you do nothing and quite possibly go through the rest of your life feeling like you have a crumb in your penis, the same way that people who lose a limb in industrial accidents go through the rest of their lives feeling like the missing limb is still there. A bit inconvenient, but certainly not anything that's going to kill you. The second option would be for me to see if I can turn anything up by way of a more thorough examination. However, a more thorough examination would involve sticking a tube right down into your penis hole, and that would probably make you faint."

In fact, the mere thought of having a tube stuck right down his penis hole had caused the man to faint; when he came to, the doctor was holding a tuna salad sandwich under his nose.

"Blech!" said the man. "Why are you holding a tuna salad sandwich under my nose?"

"Because I'd already sprinkled all my smelling salts on it," explained the doctor.

"What'd you do a stupid thing like that for?"

"I ran out of regular salt! It was either use smelling salts or eat my tuna salad sandwich without any salt on it like some sort of savage! Also, if you think that's bad, wait 'til I tell you what I used for the pepper."

But as it turned out, he couldn't tell the man anything, because the man had just died.

Ironically enough, when a subsequent postmortem revealed nothing else out of the ordinary, his official cause of death was ruled to have been "Sensation of Crumb in Penis," meaning that far as the government was concerned, feeling like he had a crumb in his penis actually had killed him.

The Snack

"I've got some bad news," a man said to another man. "Very bad."

"How bad can it be?" scoffed the second man. "After all, what doesn't kill you makes you stronger."

"Well actually," the first man said, "in this case it's going to kill you. What I mean is, you're dying."

"Hold it right there," said the second man. "Who the hell are you to just waltz on in here and tell me I'm dying?"

"Your doctor," replied the first. "And in here is my examination room, where you were waiting for me to come back and tell you about your test results, which is what I'm currently doing.."

"Fine," said the second man. "But be that as it may, in the end it's still up to God to decide whether I live or die."

"I never said it wasn't," replied the doctor. "All I'm doing is informing you of his decision."

"Hmm," said the second man. "I'm going to have to think that one over for a minute."

For a long time, he was very quiet.

Eventually the doctor looked at his watch and realized he was about to be late for his next appointment. "Hey," he said to the man who was dying. "Are you done thinking yet, because I've got a full schedule today and if I get behind now it's just going to snowball on me. Hey! Yoo-hoo! Hello!"

But the man did not answer him, because he had died.

"Well, that certainly escalated quickly," the doctor said. Then he thought that before leaving the room to call the undertakers, he should place a coin in the dead man's mouth as a bribe to ensure his safe passage across the River Styx into the kingdom of the dead or, conversely, in order to prevent his soul from escaping his dead body and spending the rest of all eternity making floorboards creak and small objects fall off of shelves in the middle of the night.

But the only coin the doctor had on hand was a chocolate one, wrapped in gold foil embossed with an image of a menorah—he must have shoved it into his pocket, he thought, during a recent Hanukkah celebration with his in-laws, who to make matters worse weren't even Jewish.

"Well," he shrugged. "Beggars can't be choosers." Then he gave the dead man a little shove so that he fell backwards onto the examining table, and carefully slid the disc of chocolate, now unwrapped, between his lips.

For a moment, it sat there balancing; a moment later, the dead man extended his tongue, took it the rest of the way into his mouth, and began to chew.

"Help!" cried the doctor. "He's alive!"

"Of course I am," said his patient, sitting up wearing a satisfied grin. "What's more, those test results you looked at were counterfeit. Yes, all this was just an elaborate scheme I cooked up for the purpose of getting a free snack, and in that regard, the only thing I can say is mission accomplished."

"Not so fast," replied the doctor. "Anticipating these dirty tricks in advance, I quickly laced that chocolate coin with poison before feeding it to you."

"Ah," said the patient. "But anticipating your anticipation, I made certain to take the antidote to that poison prior putting my plan into action."

"Cunning," said the doctor. "That said, if you think you've successfully thwarted me, you'll be surprised to learn that I brought with me to the office today my best nunchaku, with which I will now proceed to beat you to a pulp."

"Not only am I not surprised," said the patient, "I am prepared, having brought with me to the same office several Chinese throwing stars, with which I now intend to defend myself vigorously."

"Fascinating," said the doctor, "and yet, foreseeing your foresight, and well-aware of your predilection for Chinese throwing stars, I have spent the last several months training with Pedro Martínez-Fraga, head of legal affairs for the World Nunchaku Association, in the proper utilization of nunchaku for the purposes of administering a terrific beating to an enemy armed with Chinese throwing stars."

"And yet," said the patient, "expecting just such a high level of preparation on your part, I made sure to coat the razor-sharp tips of my Chinese throwing stars with human feces so that if, in the midst of this beating, I manage to inflict upon you even a single wound, severe infection requiring amputation of the affected limb, or worse, will soon develop at the site."

"Ingenious," acknowledged the doctor. "But if you think you will therefore escape this examination room unscathed, you've got another thing coming, for it just so happens that as a back-up plan to all my previous back-up plans, I hired a very large meteorite to slam into the earth, putting an instantaneous end to all human existence, in five, four, three, two..."

Fake Heart Surgeon

A man was going in for heart surgery, which all things considered was turning out to be a pretty stressful experience.

"Don't worry," the doctor told him just before the decisive dose of anesthesia was delivered. "Basically, I'm just a plumber who happens to work on arteries instead of pipes, but the basic principles are the same—get in there and clean out the gunk so things don't back up on you."

As the man's final thought before losing consciousness was that the doctor was just being self-effacing, he was as surprised as he was dismayed to discover, upon awakening several hours later, that the so-called doctor had actually been telling the truth and, to make matters worse, had totally fucked up the surgery as a result of his complete lack of relevant training.

Luckily, the man didn't die; however, his heart was left in such a condition that, according to the real doctors who picked up his case after the plumber was sent to prison, he would have to be very careful going forward in order to prevent himself from dying what would likely be a precipitous but nonetheless painful death. For example, it was no longer considered safe for him to walk up steep hills or more than two flights of stairs, engage in vigorous sexual activity with his wife, or experience strong emotions of any sort.

Consequently, whenever anyone asked him how he felt about what had happened, he would take a deep breath, count backwards from ten, and say: "I suppose it was better than if a heart surgeon had tried to fix my toilet, in any event."

4.

Stories about billboards

Preparation

A billboard not far from my place of employment, and which I therefore pass on certain early mornings when I am expected to present myself there in person, reads:

> IF YOU CAN PREPARE FOR A BIRTHDAY PARTY,
> YOU CAN PREPARE FOR AN EMERGENCY

Notwithstanding the fact that this billboard has been paid for by the state in the interest of encouraging emergency preparedness amongst its residents, I think the central claim it makes is accurate. For example, in an emergency, just like at a birthday party, one would be well-advised to have a cake on hand, in the case of the latter in order to celebrate with something sweet, while in that of the latter in order to have something to eat while waiting for the danger to pass, or—should the danger persist—to be rescued by the pertinent authorities.

Then again, if either of the aforementioned takes too long, one is liable to run out of cake—even if it's one of those large sheet cakes sold with customized frosting messages scrawled onto them by someone in a hairnet at the local supermarket—and this is precisely why, in an emergency just as at a birthday party, one will also want to have no fewer than several guests in attendance, in order that the individual whose birthday is being celebrated feel properly feted, on the one hand, and on the other in order to have something to eat after the cake is gone.

But while it has been proven on several occasions (the respective examples of the soccer team whose plane crashed in the

Andes mountains and the nineteenth century settlers trapped in the Sierra Nevada mountains in deep winter are only the most famous among them, presumably because they have been the subjects of popular films) that absent more appetizing options, people will more or less gladly resort to cannibalism, murder is a different story. For this reason, it is as advisable to hire a clown for an emergency as it is to hire a clown for a birthday party, because unlike regular people, clowns, always entertaining at birthday parties, are also naturally inclined to commit murder, from which consideration it follows that by simply promising to share with the clown in question a portion of the bounty, it would be easy to persuade him or her to murder whichever guest one had decided to eat next.

Piñatas are an important part of birthday parties in many cultures, and could equally serve one well in an emergency. What I would personally recommend is loading the piñata with a bowling ball and encouraging the person one wants to eat next to have a go at it. When the piñata splits, the bowling ball will fall directly onto that person's head, either killing them *tout suite* or knocking them unconscious and therein unable to defend themselves when the clown gets down to the business of murdering them.

In summary, I not only agree that if you can prepare for a birthday party, you can prepare for an emergency, but have now explained why.

A Most Literal Town

As part of a statewide traffic worker safety campaign, a billboard advertisement was placed along a stretch of highway bisecting a mid-sized coastal town in the northeastern United States. Like many other such billboards, placed in the context of many other such traffic worker safety campaigns, this one read:

PLEASE SLOW DOWN
MY DAD WORKS HERE

But this advertisement, rather than simply employing the typical childlike font intended to signify, without specifically identifying, the child at risk of becoming a future orphan should drivers not comply with the advertisement's request (indeed, it relied on a simple sans serif font), featured, in the white space beneath the above text, an image of an adorable puppy wearing an oversized hard hat. Needless to say, the decision to go with the puppy had only been taken by the small advertising firm to which the contract for this particular traffic worker safety campaign had been awarded in the interest of attracting the attention of the same motorists who, having seen so many similar billboard advertisements in the past, might otherwise have looked past this one. But as it happens, residents of the aforementioned town were, and still are, an extremely literal bunch; although the traffic worker safety campaign has long since been abandoned by the state in the interest of reallocating funds to the Office of Business Development, and the advertisement in question replaced with, in no particular order, an advertisement for a pawn shop, an advertisement for an adult bookstore and novelty shop, an advertisement for a casino, an advertisement for a car dealership, an advertisement for a personal injury attorney, an advertisement discouraging the abuse of illegal methamphetamines, an advertisement for a culinary tour of Italy sponsored by an area Italian restaurant ("A Taste of Italy" being the name of both tour and restaurant), and even, at a time when nobody else was paying for the space, an advertisement for the billboard itself, their search for that puppy's dad—the elusive and by-now legendary "Construction Dog," as he is known—continues to this day. In fact, during a recent visit to Pittsburgh to attend a nondenominational conference of clergypersons and other religious and spiritual leaders, the Rabbi Mordechai O'Shaughnessy was briefly convinced he had found him, working with a team preparing the infamous 16th Street Bridge for demolition. Upon closer examination, however, the affable Talmudist determined that the dog with the jackhammer was actually just a very hairy man.

5.

Stories with Animals Other Than Horses

Parrot and Me

I've said it before, and I'll say it again: I might have never lost my virginity if it hadn't been for that parrot. I was sixteen years-old and he lived in a cage in the waiting room at my orthodontist's office. What's more, he had originally belonged to my orthodontist's father, also an orthodontist, and had been passed down to my orthodontist as part and parcel of the family business. In other words, he was by then quite old; yet despite getting on in years, he still had his sheen, two clear, dry nostrils, and a pair of shining eyes. One afternoon—I kept a standing Wednesday appointment due to certain mandibular abnormalities that required me to have my orthodontia readjusted on a weekly basis—I was relaxing in the waiting room reading an article in a year-old copy of Sports Illustrated magazine about a no-longer-recent shocking turn of events in the world of professional boxing when I felt those shining eyes settle upon me.

"Hey," I said, catching them. "What are you looking at."

"What are you looking at?" asked the parrot, giving his feathers a mischievous ruffle and fluff.

"You," I answered truthfully, and—his pupils dilating—the parrot at once admitted that he had similarly been looking at me.

I glanced at the orthodontist's assistant: her attention appeared altogether occupied by an unwieldy wad of chewing gum.

"Well," I said, turning my attention back to the parrot and lowering my voice only slightly. "Do you like what you see?"

"Do you like what you see?" the parrot asked.

"I do," I said, once again truthfully. "You?"

"I do," he said. "You."

I blushed and the parrot drew his head back, bobbed it forward, and proceeded to regurgitate a great quantity of food, something anyone who knows anything about parrots knows is an unequivocal sign of affection.

From there, one thing led to another until I was completely naked and the parrot—well, the parrot had been naked all along if you don't count the feathers, and he was still naked. Needless to say, the orthodontist and his assistant had long since departed, unaware I was hiding in the storage closet, and with respect to my parents, they were under the impression I was studying for an upcoming arithmetic exam at Dennis Lad's house and would be home by midnight at the latest.

"I'm proud of you for your effort," my mother had said from the other end of the line when I lied to her, adding that she'd always known I had it in me to do my best in school.

Now, of course, school—and my mother—were the furthest thing from my mind.

"Are you sure you want to do this?" I asked the parrot.

"Are you sure you want to do this?" the parrot, ever deferential, replied.

I closed my eyes and breathed in his salty scent, reminiscent of gym shorts left too many days without washing in a closed locker. "My answer," I said, opening them again, "is yes."

"*My* answer," replied the parrot, "is yes."

At that, I unlatched the cage's little door and allowed it to swing open; without further delay, the parrot hopped through, beat his wings once, uselessly, in the air, and floated in for a soft landing at my feet. The hours spread out before us like a holiday feast.

+

The following Wednesday, when I returned for my regularly scheduled appointment, the birdcage, along with its occupant, was gone.

“Hng appfle ugh grr phrrrrt?” I asked the orthodontist.

“Come again,” he said, removing his husky hands from my mouth.

“I was wondering what happened to the parrot,” I repeated.

For a moment, the mustachioed jawsmith regarded me gravely, and as though with suspicion; then he said, “Don’t talk to me about that slut,” and reached for a rather brutal looking pair of Weingart pliers.

Story with a Joke

While visiting his in-laws for the holidays, a man dreamed the following joke:

> *Question:* What's another way of saying "change the color of a rare South American bird distantly related to the ostrich and emu, using a natural or synthetic pigment-altering substance?"
> *Answer:* Dye a rhea.

Pleased with the labors of his subconscious, in the days that followed the man shared this joke with as many of his friends and family members as he could track down (pretty much all of them). To his surprise, however, no one laughed—worse, most people did not react at all, with the exception of the man's second cousin's husband, who responded with a look of confusion, probably because the dunce didn't even know what a rhea was, as well as the man's great aunt, who turned as red as a rose and asked him to kindly keep his "bathroom humor" out of her home.

Convinced the joke deserved better, the man set out in search of a more receptive audience, leaving behind his wife and children without so much as a note on the kitchen table. After years of wandering, following an improvised itinerary that took him to Timbuktu and back again, metaphorically speaking and also literally, the man settled at last upon a certain former circus kangaroo residing near the Russian border with Outer Mongolia, these days better known as Mongolia. Unfortunately for the man, the reason this particular kangaroo had enjoyed the long and lucrative career in the circus from which he was now retired was precisely that he was one of those muscular boxing kangaroos who would gladly take on all challengers, no matter how hairy and burly, and had moreover never been defeated in the ring. Thus, while the kangaroo did, in fact, laugh at the man's joke—specifically, what he said was, "Ha ha, as in diarrhea, I get it"—he also punched him so hard in the stomach that, like poor Harry Houdini, the man soon died of peritonitis caused by a ruptured appendix.

Then again, maybe none of that ever actually happened because, having foreseen it all, the man decided a wiser course of action would be to write the little story you're currently reading and send it out into the world in the hopes that, along with the joke it contains, it might eventually make its own way to that Mongolian kangaroo. Therefore, if you happen to see him, please do pass it along.

Rodent Disposal

Recently, a mouse was in my house. It was a very small, very deceased mouse, discovered by my wife in the middle of the basement floor, which is pretty much just a big slab of concrete. The mouse had a placid look about it and showed no signs of violence; all the same, it appeared to have leaked blood in a way that made the whole situation resemble the scene of a very gentle crime. Wearing a glove, I picked the dead mouse up by the tail—I had to tug a bit harder than I'd anticipated, because the blood that had leaked from it was acting as an adhesive—and deposited it in one bag, and that bag in a second bag, and the pair of bags in the garbage dumpster in the garage, where it will be collected this coming Tuesday by the trash collectors, and taken by the trash collectors to a dump or a landfill, or perhaps a dump and from there to a landfill, where for reasons I still don't fully comprehend it will decompose much more slowly than it would have if, for example, I'd simply buried it in the garden. In fact, I probably would have simply buried it the garden if not for the fact that the possibility did not occur to me until just now.

Speaking of dead mice, I am reminded of the time, many years ago by now, that my family home was infiltrated by a very large mouse. The reason it was so large was that, according to the exterminator my father summoned to take care of it, it was actually a very small rat—a tree rat, to be exact, which depending on the circumstances has also been known to be referred to as a black rat, house rat, ship rat, or roof rat (why, considering that it was quite literally in our house, the exterminator chose to refer to it as a "tree rat" rather than a "house rat" is another question altogether). The exterminator, who I remember having blond hair and the smell of furniture that once got wet, managed to flush the rat out from where it taken refuge behind the living room couch, and then he chased it from room to room wielding a long pole with a kind of grabbers or pincers at the end. This went on for a given period of time until, breathless and perspiring, he informed us that he was going try a different tactic. Specifically, this tactic involved setting out glue traps in various strategic locations throughout the house and then, once having collected a sum of money as payment that could as easily be considered modest as exorbitant depending on one's perspective, going on his way.

Wherever he was going, he could not have gotten far when a scuffling behind the living room couch alerted us that the rat had been trapped. And indeed, there it was, trying to free itself and then looking briefly resigned to its fate before trying to free itself again. At that point my father called the exterminator, who congratulated him on his catch.

"Thanks," my father replied. "But what am I supposed to do with it now?"

"Ah," said the exterminator. "Basically, you can either toss it into the trash where it will die a slow, excruciating death, probably ripping its legs from its body and disemboweling itself in the process, or you could choose to go the humane route and club it to death before putting it in the trash."

"I don't think I would be capable of doing that," my father told him.

"In that case," the exterminator suggested, "a third option would be to take it to a country road somewhere and run over it with your car. I'd tell you to just go ahead and do it in your driveway, but it can be hard to get the stains out of the concrete, and if you do it out on the street, I don't technically think that would be legal, so that's why I'm suggesting a country road."

"I don't think I would be capable of doing that, either," my father replied.

"No problem," said the exterminator. "You can always put it in a pillowcase and beat it against a tree."

"Yeah," my father said. "I don't think I would be capable of doing that, either."

"You could drown it," suggested the exterminator.

"Actually, I couldn't," said my father.

"Then boil it," said the exterminator.

"Nope," said my father.

"I've got it," said the exterminator. "Stick a firecracker up its ass, light the fuse, and get the hell out of the way."

But while it was legal in our state to possess fireworks, it was illegal to buy them, sell them, barter with them, or give or receive them as gifts, meaning that, having none of our own at the time, we also had no way of acquiring any.

Fran, Who Became a Crow

After his wife left him for a handsome co-worker with an electric car, Fran decided to take up downhill skiing. At first, everything seemed to be going well, and Fran even allowed himself to imagine meeting the next love his life while attending an Après-ski Three Dog Night tribute concert back at the lodge. But then, coming upon an unexpectedly steep section of trail while descending an otherwise gentle slope that traversed the outer edge of the mountain (he was a beginner, after all), Fran lost control of his momentum, careened through the rather flimsy barrier that had been erected there, and tumbled head over heels into what, for lack of a better word, we might as well just go ahead and refer to as the abyss.

As a young child contending for the first time with the impossible inevitability of his own mortality, it so happens that Fran had formulated a certain fantasy as a kind of intellectual and emotional workaround. Specifically, he imagined that when he was old and infirm, instead of just lying down and dying the way old and infirm people so often do, he would have a willing relative—for instance, a son or, more likely, a grandson or great nephew—push him to the top of a mountain in his wheelchair (he took for granted that he would be confined to a wheelchair by then) and shove him over the edge. Then, he imagined, to the amazement of his son or grandson or great nephew or whoever it was who'd taken him there and shoved him over the edge, rather than falling to his death he would magically transform into a bird (the wheelchair, meanwhile, would keep on falling) and soar off, glorious and alive, into the sky-blue distance.

Now, albeit in slightly different circumstances, Fran really had just gone off a cliff, and amazingly enough, the thing he'd so long ago imagined actually happened. To put it otherwise, rather than feeling his stomach drop, as one plunging through thin air would expect, Fran felt his wings—wings!—spread wide, and he felt the weight of the air beneath him, and his body, as light as a feather (a bundle of feathers, to be exact), surfing on the wind.

"Holy shit!" he screamed. "It's a miracle!"

Well, at least that was what he intended to scream. In reality, what came out of his mouth—that is, his beak—was: "Caw! Caw! Caw, caw, caw!"

Could it be that of all the birds in the world into which he might have been transformed, he had been transformed into a lowly crow? It seemed so, for suddenly he was overcome by an overwhelming appetite for trash. Just the thought of it was making his mouth—that is, his beak—water. Luckily, it was an easy problem to solve: he simply drifted down to where a half-dozen dumpsters were lined up in the little alleyway behind the lodge, and soon enough he was feasting on a heap of half-frozen French fries caked in congealed ketchup, followed by a dirty napkin and what may or may not have been a cigarette butt (smoking was forbidden at the ski resort, but it sure tasted like a cigarette butt). Everything was delicious, but at the same time Fran was repulsed by the pleasure he was taking in it, which must have been, he reflected, the way certain sexual deviants felt when indulging appetites of a decidedly different variety, though in recognizing this, he reminded himself, he was in no way was excusing their deviant behavior if and when it ran afoul of the law, although on further consideration he wondered whether he was too hastily granting the law—when all is said and done, a mechanism for the reification state power—the moral authority it so eagerly claims for itself. He would have given more thought to this complicated matter, but just then the back door of the lodge swung open, and a man clad in dishwashing attire burst through it, as wild-eyed as a dervish, swinging a broom in Fran's direction and shouting, "Shoo! Shoo, you vile blight, shoo!"

With a pair of hops and a series of quick flaps of his wings, Fran easily evaded the assault. But as he ascended, it occurred to him that, all things considered, it might be more interesting to find out what death was like than it would be to live out a second life as a trash-eating crow, disdained by his formerly fellow humans. With that in mind, he located the cliff at the top of the mountain with the sheerest drop, hopped to the edge, recited a few Hail Marys and a Mourner's Kaddish for good measure, and for the second time that afternoon, tumbled into the abyss.

Being that his intention was to die, Fran naturally told himself not to flap his wings. But it turned out that telling himself not to flap his wings was basically like that time back in college when he came out of the library one night to find that someone had stolen his bicycle seat and as he climbed aboard to ride back to the dorms his good buddy told him, "Whatever you do, bro, don't sit down." In other words, he did it anyway. Turning a few halfhearted circles, he contemplated additional possibilities for committing what he didn't exactly consider suicide, seeing as technically he should have been dead already, but none of those possibilities seemed any more promising. Take hanging, for example: how would he set up a rope with which to hang himself (and even if he could, how would he the fasten that rope around his neck, etc.) with those weird little bird feet-hands of his? He ran into the same problem when he pondered shooting himself in the heart, or locking himself inside an idling motor vehicle in a closed garage. And though a falling piano would certainly do him in, how, in his current form, was he going to figure out where and when someone was planning to push a piano out of a tenth-story window?

Seeing no other option, he finally resolved to just go ahead and try and make the best of his situation, which is precisely why you can these days find him living in a tall tree at the edge of the small, wooded area behind the house his ex-wife shares with her handsome new husband, driving the two of them completely crazy with his non-stop fucking cawing.

Two Pregnancies

A crabby woman was pregnant and crabby about it.

"I hate being pregnant!" she kept saying. "I wish I could just lay an egg and make him (meaning her husband) sit on it!"

She wished this wish so hard that eventually it came true: when she gave birth, what slid out was not a human baby, as she and her husband and basically everyone else in the room was expecting, but rather a smooth, shiny egg, approximately 1.5 times the size of an ostrich egg.

"Great," said the crabby woman, regarding it. "I really did lay a fucking egg, but I still ended up having to be pregnant for nine months. At least I won't have to start breastfeeding, anyway."

"I would recommend sitting on it," said the doctor on call. "I don't know a ton about eggs, but I know they're meant to be sat on."

"That's all you," the crabby woman said to her husband.

Luckily, the man was more than happy to oblige since he led a very sedentary life to begin with, primarily owing to the fact that he had no legs.

In this way, several weeks passed during which the crabby woman's husband sat faithfully on the egg she had laid. Although she was quite crabby about it, the crabby woman brought him his meals and cleared away the dishes when he was finished eating, and at night she propped a few extra pillows behind him so he could get a little sleep. The rest of the time she watched movies, played word games on her mobile phone, and attended exercise classes and various other activities mainly involving other women in her age group and general demographic.

Then, one otherwise unremarkable day, the man felt something moving inside the egg. And then he heard something—peck, peck, peck. And then he heard something else: craaa-aaack!

"Honey!" he cried. "It's hatching!"

But his crabby wife was off at a Pilates class, or else she might have been at one of those places where you drink wine and do something artistic, like make a painting or throw a ceramic pot, in which case she might have been saying, at the very moment the man was calling out to her: "This is turning out like shit, the same as everything else in my life."

Meanwhile, bits and pieces of the egg were flying around the room until at last, a hole had been opened up that was big enough for whatever was inside of it to come crawling out—or, in this case, rolling out, for as it turned out, what had hatched was none other than a 1978 Ford Bronco with tinted windows.

I know what you're probably thinking at this juncture: a 1978 Ford Bronco with tinted windows actually would have been pretty cool if only that man had had some legs with which to drive it. Well, I've got news for you—I was totally bullshitting earlier when I said he didn't have any legs. In reality, he had a perfectly functional pair of legs, which he proceeded to put to good use driving his newborn Bronco up and down Main Street all day long, pretty much every day and usually well into the evening, too. In fact, that was how he eventually met Lola, who was brand new in town and just walking out of the local diner, where she'd applied for a job.

"Cool truck," she observed as the man cruised on by.

"Why don't you come check out the inside of it, in that case?" the man replied.

No one knows for certain what happened behind those tinted windows, being that you can't see through them, but what we do know is that five months later, in the very same hospital in which his crabby ex-wife had laid an egg, the man's new wife, Lola from the diner, gave birth to a beautiful baby goat.

6.

Stories the Titles of Which Begin with "The"

The Ice Skater

Marvin was certain he was good at something; unfortunately, others were equally certain he was not.

Specifically, the thing he was certain he was good at but others were certain he was not was ice skating, and even more specifically, comfortably gliding backwards over a distance roughly equal to his height while ice skating. You see, in the interest of self-improvement, Marvin had enrolled in an ice-skating program at his local YMCA, and in order to pass from Level 1 to Level 2 at the end of the first six-week session, he was required to demonstrate proficiency in a number of skills, including the aforementioned gliding backwards over a distance roughly equal to his height. While he was judged proficient in all other relevant skills, the instructor in charge of assessments at the end of the first session deemed him insufficiently so in his backwards gliding, and notified Marvin that, should he elect to continue with the program, he would therefore be required to repeat Level 1 in its entirety. Upon receiving the news, Marvin declared the instructor a charlatan and a skank and demanded a second opinion, which he subsequently received from another instructor who similarly deemed him insufficiently proficient with respect to his backwards gliding, and for good measure—or more likely, Marvin thought, out of spite—added that he had significant room for improvement when it came to his left-foot forward glides.

Marvin sought comfort in the arms of his friends.

"Oh, Marvin," they told him. "It's just one person's opinion."

"Two," Marvin reminded them.

"Anyway," they said, "maybe it's all for the best, because if you got too advanced at ice skating at this point in your life, it would honestly be kind of weird. Like, why would you even want to get that good at ice skating—it's not like you're going to make the Olympics? Plus, ice skating itself is weird. I mean, what dumbass Einstein came up with genius idea to glue knives to the bottoms of a pair of shoes and then trying to walk around in them on planet earth's slipperiest surface?"

"Thanks for the input," Marvin said. Then he went back to his basement apartment, put his ice skates in the oven, and set them to bake at 500 degrees. While the skates slowly transformed into slurry of stinking toxic ash and scorched metal, Marvin placed a call to the instructor who had initially deemed him insufficiently proficient in his backward glides—the one he had called a charlatan and a skank—and invited her over for sexual intercourse.

"Normally I'd say no," she told him. "However, on the grounds that I've been putting so much time and energy into lowering people's self-esteem by way of ice skating that I can hardly remember what it feels like to indulge the pleasures of the flesh, I'm going to accept the invitation."

Thirty minutes later, their intimate congress had already reached its terminus.

Marvin rolled onto his back and fixed his gaze on a water stain on the ceiling that, he'd long been convinced, looked exactly like the late Jimi Hendrix. "So," he said. "Was it as good for you as it was for me?"

"No," the ice-skating instructor replied dryly.

"Well," said Marvin, "since it was super shitty for me, I'll take that as a compliment."

The Man Who Was in Danger of Becoming Wayward

A man, upon reaching early middle age without having established himself in a career or started a family, was informed by his friends that he was in danger of becoming wayward.

"But how do I change course?" asked the man, who could clearly see the disadvantages inherent in such a fate.

One of his friends, an infamous go-getter with an infectious can-do spirit, told him, "There actually happens to be an exceedingly simple formula for this. First, you figure out what you really want in life. Then, you make a plan for how to get it. Then, you stick to that plan. Every. Single. Day."

"Very inspiring," said the man who was in danger of becoming wayward. "But how am I supposed to figure out what I really want in life?"

"I'm afraid I can't help you with that one," said his friend with the can-do spirit, and scurried off.

Subsequently, the man paid a visit to the local self-help guru, a slender but muscular gentleman with a long beard, no shirt, and several tattoos of a nondenominationally spiritual nature, whose services helping people figure out what they really wanted in life were, according to the promotional literature he had distributed to various coffee shops, vegetarian restaurants, and used bookstores throughout the greater metropolitan area, accompanied by a money-back guarantee.

"Yes, yes," nodded the guru when the man in danger of becoming wayward detailed his plight. Then he gave his beard a few tugs and said: "The way I see things, we could start you off with some testicular tanning or, of course, a series of primal screams. But based on the vibrations I've been picking up during our short time together, I'm feeling pretty confident that in your particular case, heading straight for the ice bath is going to be the best solution."

"What's an ice bath?" asked the man.

"Follow me," the guru instructed him.

In the yard behind the guru's house, most of the rooms in which had been rented out to various neighborhood good-for-nothings, there was—along with a concrete bust of the Buddha draped in green and purple Mardi Gras beads—a large barrel made of thick plastic.

"This barrel," explained the guru, "is filled with freezing cold ice water, which I guess all ice water is since otherwise it technically wouldn't be ice water. Anyway, the point is, what you're going to do is get in and submerge yourself up to the neck."

"For how long?" asked the man.

"As long as it takes," replied the guru.

"Well, you're the guru in this relationship, I suppose." The man stripped down to his undergarments and stepped into the barrel—standing, the water reached his waist.

"Holy shit," he gasped. "Are you sure this is safe?"

"As safe as driving a car..." said the guru.

"If you say so." The man took a deep breath and slowly lowered himself, grunting and grimacing, until the water reached his chin.

"... the wrong way down the freeway in the middle of the night at a hundred miles an hour with your headlights turned off," the guru continued.

"What!?" said the man.

"Hypothermia, shock, sudden cardiac arrest," said the guru.

"There's a reason ice baths are considered a highly controversial treatment. I haven't personally witnessed any of those adverse outcomes, but then again, this is my first time actually using the thing on anyone."

"What!?" said the man.

"Yeah," said the guru. "I just got it yesterday at the Home Depot down on Seven Mile Road. Scratch and dent sale type of situation. I would have tried it out myself, but I've always been extremely sensitive to cold water. Even in the middle of the summer, you can find me taking a piping hot shower. And in the winter, forget about it. My bathroom is like one of those steam chambers where deviant Europeans go to exchange anonymous intimacies with one another."

"That's it," said the man, clambering out of the barrel and gathering up his clothes. "You're nothing but a con artist and a quack."

"I'm sorry you feel that way," said the guru. "Do you want your money back?"

"Yes," said the man.

"Do you really?" asked the guru.

"Yes!" shouted the man.

On the grounds that, this being the case, he had in fact performed precisely the service for which he had been hired, the guru denied the request.

The Impressive Observation

Squeezing a dollop of soap out of the dispenser beside the bathroom sink, a man who had just enjoyed his morning elimination noticed that it slid into the palm of his hand having assumed the shape of a scrotum encasing a well-balanced pair of testicles. He shared this observation with his wife, who—still in bed—replied:

"On a scale of one to a thousand, how impressed with yourself would you say you are right now?"

"A thousand," the man said without thinking twice. "What about you?"

"A thousand," said his wife, rolling over. "A thousand plus."

Next, the man called the high school teacher who, in a fit of pique regarding an incident involving a fake monkey, a bucket of sodium bicarbonate, and several jars of raspberry jam, once assured him he would never amount to anything.

"Wow," said the teacher, who must have been pretty elderly by now, per the man's back-of-the-napkin math. "I've been wrong about my students before but never to a major extreme such as this one. Talk about having egg on your face. With a spatula and a spritz or two of Pam Original No-Stick Cooking Spray, you could easily make an omelet out of me. Ideally with a little shredded cheese and some diced peppers, but then again, that's ultimately a matter personal preference. Anyway, I've got to get back to being an old piece of shit who's probably going to die soon, but I really do appreciate you taking time of out of your busy day to let me know just what a moron I was for underestimating you like that all those years ago."

Even the soap itself was impressed. "Pretty perceptive," it

said to the man when he told him what he'd observed. "I honestly wasn't expecting anyone to notice that about me."

Then the man opened the tap and rubbed his hands together under the spray of water, and it foamed up and ran off down the drain saying "glub, glub, glub."

The Last Men on Earth

Two men spent their lives arguing over an abstract matter in which moral or ethical principles were implicated. They were not arguing about whether the deployment of the atomic bomb in the Second World War was justified, but this is an example of the sort of thing they were arguing about.

When they were young, as is the habit of youth, the two men argued from their passions. They proclaimed their commitment to categorical imperatives, evoked images of women and children raped and mangled, of the yellow stars Jews in Germany and German-occupied territories were obligated to pin to their shirts under the Nazi regime, of flood and plague; they traded accusations of the worst sort, though (not literally, needless to say) each knew perfectly well the other wouldn't hurt a fly. In their middle years, the long, long middle years, the men moved on to arguing from research and reason, or so they wanted to believe. They wielded statistics, cited historical precedent, constructed approximations of syllogisms from which they were each time convinced there could be no reasonable escape, but then the other always seemed to find a hatch, or at least to think he had. Later, as they transitioned into old age, the men argued, heads held high, from the wisdom of experience, prefacing their propositions with phrases such as, "As I've gotten older, one thing I've realized is..." and, "Looking back, one thing I can see now is that..." Finally, as they drifted into what we might call the homestretch, they enlisted their own impending doom as rhetorical guarantor. "I've got no horse left in this race," they would say, as though a point of view argued from a position of disinterest could not be wrong (and yet each insisted the other's was).

In some ways, the argument between these two men didn't just span their lives but shaped them, and not necessarily for the better. If they hadn't been so preoccupied with bringing the other around to their position, for instance, maybe they would have focused more on their schoolwork, and achieved better results and, with those better results, found more fulfilling or more handsomely remunerated jobs; if they hadn't been busy formulating their rejoinder to their opponent's most recent rejoinder, they might have performed better in the jobs they did find, and those jobs may have even turned into what could more properly be thought of as a career, and those careers, in turn, into lake houses, investment accounts, unforgettable vacations to far flung territories; and if they'd held to it, just once, when they said, before saying whatever it was they wanted to say, "This is the last thing I'm going to say on the matter," perhaps they would have been more present to their wives and their families, and one of them wouldn't have ended up divorced, nor the other treated like an unpleasant chore by the only of his three children who still came to visit him in the assisted living facility in which he shared a room, per their mutual request, with his lifelong adversary, so that they could continue to argue with one other, each from the narrow bed above which dangled the string he pulled to ring the bell that summoned the nurse.

At last, death came calling—walking down the hall, scythe in hand. Hearing its footsteps, one of the men—it doesn't matter which—turned to the other and spoke what would turn out to have been his final words: "You know, the more I think about it, the more I think you might actually be right."

And with his dying breath, the other replied: "Actually, bro, you have some really good points, too."

The Lovelorn Leg

A particular man applied to his injured leg an analgesic cream containing, as a secondary ingredient serving a primarily emulsifying purpose, a substance celebrated within certain homeopathic and otherwise non-traditional medical circles for its properties as an aphrodisiac. Soon, the leg developed feelings toward the man that were not reciprocated, and from there the situation rapidly deteriorated: wherever the man went, the leg was right there with him, and while the man wasn't a mean person by nature, he constantly found himself being mean to the leg simply because being nice to it risked giving off a false impression, which was actually kind of mean in its own right because then the leg would end up getting its hopes up only to have them dashed all over again. Seeing that there was nothing else to be done, the man fetched his hacksaw from the cellar and a couple of rags from the basket underneath the kitchen sink and headed for the garage.

Alas, it was all a terrible mistake—hardly had the man rid himself of the irksome appendage when he realized that in reality, he was the one who could not live without it and not the other way around.

He decided to swallow his pride and go crawling back, but you can imagine how well that worked out.

The Man Who Thought He Was in Love but Then Thought Better of It

"Toot, toot," called out the approaching train.

A man and woman were walking arm-in-arm through the thick cover of autumn leaves that had fallen on either side of the tracks, their pants tucked into their socks to protect against the ticks, which in recent years seemed to have become more of a scourge than ever in the arboreous zone they called home.

"What do you want me to do to prove it?" the man inquired of the woman, who—either in spite of the fact that she quite fancied him, or because of it—had just received his florid declarations of love with skepticism. "Should I climb the highest mountain? Swim the deepest sea? Should I ritualistically sacrifice my own son like Isaac on the Temple Mount, which would be impossible since I don't currently have a son but if you give me a little time, I could probably adopt one and then ritualistically sacrifice him?"

"Thanks, but no thanks to those old chestnuts," replied the woman. "How about doing something original like throwing yourself in front of that oncoming train."

"Your wish is my command," declared the man, and hopped into its path.

"TOOT! TOOT!" the train blared.

Then, *kablooey*—as he leapt to safety at the very last moment, the water balloon the man had been carrying with him in case a water balloon fight randomly broke out slipped from his pocket, splattering against the forest floor.

7.

Stories about Food, and also Death

The Man Who Was Considering Soaking his Own Beans

"You buy them dry," he told his friend. "Then you soak them until they're ready to cook."

"That sounds like a real pain in the ass," his friend observed. "You have to plan your bean eating what, thirty-six hours in advance? Who's going to do that?"

"Good point," the man conceded. "But on the other hand, if you happen to find yourself in a conversation about beans, you can say, *I actually buy them dry and soak them myself.*"

"Hmm," said his friend.

He wasn't totally convinced, but you could tell he was coming around.

Too Much Cheese

Somehow, I ended up with a tremendous quantity of cubed cheese.

I say somehow, but I know how—I just don't really want to get into it. In any event, the question now was how to get rid of it.

I started with my friend who is known above all for his love of cheese and a willingness to consume it in great quantities.

"No can do," he said. "Cholesterol."

I could hardly believe it—he was thin, an avid racquetball player, and ate fish at least once a week, but never more than twice.

"I think it must have been all that cheese," he explained. "Either that or bad genes. But of the two, there's only one I can do something about, and that's the cheese. You know that the majority of fatal heart attacks aren't the result of arterial blockage, right? Eighty percent of the time, what happens is that an unstable plaque in one of the arteries bursts, and then a clot forms around it, and from there—goodnight, Irene. In case you haven't figured it out, I'm Irene in this example."

"You think you've got problems," I said. "What the hell am I supposed to do with all this cubed cheese?"

"You're a very creative person," he said. "I'm sure you'll think of something."

What I thought of was to leave it on a card table near my apartment building's first-floor elevator, but that didn't work out because none of the other tenants were interested, apparently due to hygiene-related concerns.

With that in mind, I bought a box of cocktail toothpicks with the little plastic frill on one end and left them, along with a small bin for their disposal, right beside the cheese. But a terrible heatwave was in progress, and everyone was sweating from every part of their body, including the wrists. To make a long story short, my fellow tenants were convinced that spearing the cheese with a toothpick instead of grabbing it with a bare hand wouldn't keep the sweat from dribbling off one's wrist into the remaining cheese, such that any piece of cheese they speared would likely have been contaminated already with someone else's wrist sweat.

They had a point, I had to admit; but in the meantime, the cheese was starting to mold. That's when I realized there was nothing for me to do but eat it myself, all of it, and moreover as quickly as I could.

"Watch out," my friends warned me. "You do something like that, you're going to end up turning into a big piece of cheese."

I thought they were wrong, but they were right! And what do you do once you've turned into a big piece of cheese? The best you can. In my case, that means offering my services as an edible cheese sculpture at fancy parties. I attend these parties, keeping very still and enjoying the ambience. Mostly, I am ignored, but from time to time someone hacks off a small piece of me and eats it.

In this way, I am slowly disappearing.

A Passion for Pork

A man with a passion for pork—a true pork lover, as it were—was driving down a two-lane highway when he spied, posted on the lawn in front of an otherwise unremarkable house, a sign announcing:

PORK FOR SALE

At once, the man pulled to the side of the road in a reckless fashion and jogged up the walk to knock at the front door, where he was attended to by the pork seller himself—a gentleman dressed in a manner that can best be described by saying his outfit was appropriately topped off by a hickory-striped engineer's cap.

"So, what kind of pork is it?" the man asked him without further preamble. "Free range? From swine nourished exclusively with acorns in the manner of Spain's famous *jamones de bellota*? Better yet, free range and from swine nourished exclusively with acorns in the manner of Spain's famous *jamones de bellota*?"

"No, no, nothing like that," replied the pork seller. "Honestly, it's just some pork I bought from the supermarket that, being a strict vegetarian, I've ended up not having much use for, and which I therefore thought I'd pass on to someone more likely to make the most of its virtues."

"I see," said the pork lover. "And are you offering it at a discount relative to its original retail price?"

The pork seller cleared his throat. "I mean, it hasn't been used at all, so I don't really see any grounds for that. That said, I suppose I could offer it to you untaxed."

"I see," repeated the pork lover. In fact, he strongly believed that, much like a brand-new car the moment it's been driven off the sales lot, a portion of supermarket pork once removed from the supermarket automatically loses between nine and eleven percent of its value. Furthermore, he was perfectly aware that in the specific state in which the current transaction was taking place, groceries were not taxed in the first place, which is to say, the pork seller was playing him for the fool with this so-called offer of his.

All the same, so powerful and unbridled was the pork lover's passion for pork that he simply could not say no.

"I simply cannot say no," he therefore said.

At that, the pork seller retreated into the darkness of his abode, momentarily returning with the pork in question—a shoulder cut, neatly packaged.

"A fine specimen," observed our protagonist.

But as he did not remember to check the expiration date on the package before stopping off at a nearby park to first fricassee its contents over the little blue flame produced by a propane camp stove he kept in the trunk of his car for just such a purpose, and then consume them with a surplus of gusto that more than compensated for his lack of cutlery, the poor fellow contracted a nasty case of trichinosis thanks to which his face is now as swollen as a puff pastry.

Breadsticks

As the result of an emerging medical condition, a man was compelled to switch from an unrestricted to a restricted diet. This was how he became familiar with a certain brand of Italian breadsticks which, being manufactured with olive oil as opposed to the more noxious lards and fats he was now prohibited from consuming, struck him as a potentially acceptable replacement for the crunchy snacks to which he had grown accustomed over the years.

But the breadsticks turned out to be much more than a merely "acceptable replacement"—rich in flavor, light and airy on the inside and baked to crispy perfection on the outside, they were in fact the most delicious food he had ever eaten, and on their own redoubled his commitment to abide by the restrictions that had been imposed on his diet insofar as the very prospect of being able to continue eating them for as long as he did motivated him to do whatever it took to go on living for as long as he could.

One specific example of how much the man loved these breadsticks was when, in the middle of the night, he was awakened from a deep sleep by the sounds of his dog threatening to vomit. At once, he got out of bed, pulling on whatever items of clothing he found closest at hand, and prepared to take the dog outside to the backyard in order that, should he vomit, he would do it there, where some vermin would surely have feasted upon it by morning. But on his way to the back door, the man could not resist taking a detour into the kitchen to help himself to an Italian breadstick or two (ultimately, he helped himself to three). In other words, he willingly increased the chances of his dog vomiting inside the house, where the vomitus would produce a foul stench and he would be obligated to sop it up with rags and paper towels, all for the pleasure of eating Italian breadsticks at a time when he would normally not be eating anything at all.

Another example of how much the man loved the breadsticks was when, on another night, his wife tossed her magazine to the floor, switched off her beside lamp, and undertook to make advances upon him.

"What's this?" said the man with surprise. "Usually, you're as frigid as a fjord."

"I think I must be reaching late middle age," his wife purred, "for I suddenly seem to have developed the relentless sexual urges so often associated with that particular stage of a woman's life."

The man drew a breath. "Look," he said. "I hate to disappoint you, because God knows I'm all too familiar what it feels like to get shut down in these situations, but at the moment, I only have feelings for my delicious Italian breadsticks. What I'm trying to say is, there's not room in my heart or, for that matter, my loins, for anyone else, including you."

"Well, that's going to be a big ass problem," said the man's wife, "because I'm so horny that I'll seriously freak out if I don't get my rocks off soon."

The man thought it over.

"Maybe if you were somehow more similar to the breadsticks—"

"Done," said his wife, lumbering out of bed.

Not five minutes later, she returned, slathered from head to toe in olive oil.

"Well?" she said.

"I see what you're getting at," said the man, "but it just doesn't seem to be working. Look for yourself—I'm as soft as pudding."

"Hmm," said his wife. "What if I went a step further and also baked myself to crispy perfection?"

"I don't want to over-promise," replied the man, "but if you're genuinely as horny as you say you are, I suppose it's at least worth a try. After all, what's the worst that could happen?"

This time, when his wife returned to the bedroom, the man took one look at her exquisitely browned flesh and became extremely aroused and, as such, fully prepared to satisfy her urges as well as his own.

Unfortunately, it so happened that in the process of baking herself to crispy perfection, the woman had—altogether predictably, the man now realized—also become deceased, meaning that to engage in any form of sexual activity with her would have been to commit necrophilia, a felony crime punishable by as many as ten years in federal prison. This being the case, the man instead dedicated the next several hours to writing her obituary.

In lieu of flowers, he requested breadsticks.

Muffins

A man made a thing.

"This is good," he said, regarding it.

But apparently, not everyone agreed.

"What???" asked one person, rhetorically.

"Pure stupidity," remarked another, as though this were not an opinion but merely an observation.

"Just when you thought it was safe to leave the house," griped a third.

At least the man's mother was proud of him.

"I'm proud of you, son," she said.

For a moment, the man felt better about the whole situation as a result of these kind words; but a moment later he realized he had to be dreaming insofar as: a.) his mother was dead; and b.) in life, she was an unforgiving woman who called him "bonehead," "nitwit," and "unplanned," and was fond of saying "tell me how much someone's willing to pay you for it and I'll tell you what it's worth."

Furthermore, even if someone had been willing to pay the man a lot of money for the thing he'd made (which, to be clear, nobody was), his mother still probably wouldn't have been proud of him for it, since it so happens that the specific thing he'd made was a batch of muffins from her ashes.

Oh, I'm only kidding—this man hated muffins!

Rest Stop

Often, people visit highway rest stops because they need to use the restrooms from which they take their name, but in this case my primary purpose (though I did use the restroom, seeing as I was there and it was there and so on) was to acquire a Coca-Cola, the reason being that I had been quite nearly falling asleep at the wheel, a dangerous proposition at any speed but especially at highway speeds, and as it happens, when I am quite nearly falling asleep at the wheel only a Coca-Cola will wake me up—coffee, for example, is useless. Well, this particular rest stop was home to, in addition to its restrooms, a convenience store and various fast-food restaurants, only two of which were open, presumably due to a tight labor market. I went first to the convenience store, where I found only one register open—also owing to the tight labor market, I surmised—and an interminable line, and inasmuch as I intended for this visit to the rest stop to be brief, as one does, I preferred not to stand there interminably, waiting to make my modest purchase.

Yet and still, returning to the car without a Coca-Cola could well have been a death sentence, and I also preferred not to die, and certainly not while sleeping at the wheel like some sort of dotard. I considered losing all hope; then it occurred to me that the restaurants at the rest stop probably also sold Coca-Cola, and as there was no line at either of them I went directly to the one nearest the convenience store, where my hunch was corroborated: in a refrigerated cooler in front of the counter, beside heaps of premade salads and sandwiches, were bottled beverages lined up like soldiers in the long slog against dehydration and sluggishness, among them several Coca-Colas. I placed one of these Coca-Colas on the counter and was promptly attended to by a gentleman about whom I can't say much because there is not much to say: he was regular by all accounts, neither young nor old, handsome nor homely, tall nor short, etc. When our transaction was completed, and the Coca-Cola safely in hand, I thanked him, to which expression of gratitude he replied: "You got it, boss."

But here's the problem: I do not like to be called "boss." In situations in which one might call me "boss," my strong preference is to be called "chief" or "home slice" or, should my interlocutor be amenable to neither of the foregoing, as a last resort "broseph." I calmly explained all of this to the gentleman with whom I had just transacted, raising neither voice nor fist, and then asked that in deference to my predilections, he repeat his farewell, now replacing "boss" with one of the approved sobriquets. Perhaps also owing to the tight labor market, which undoubtedly makes it difficult to fire someone for the sorts of indiscretions for which they in other times would have been dismissed posthaste, the gentleman not only obstinately refused to accommodate my request but did so in an overtly hostile matter. Specifically, what he said was: "I'll call you whatever the fuck I want... boss."

Well, this was too much, just far too much. If he'd simply denied my request, even with hostility, I may have let it pass, but to call me boss again, and moreover after a dramatic pause—no, it was just far, far too much. With vengeance on my mind, I grabbed one of the prepackaged salads from the cooler, opened it, and poured it right onto the gentleman's head, showering him in lettuce and croutons and fatty clumps of ranch dressing. In response, he clouted me repeatedly with a bag of frozen Italian meatballs—it must have been close at hand—before tearing the bag open and emptying its contents onto my own head. Stinking of parsley, basil, and beef, I leapt over the counter by which we had until then been separated, picked up a pile of onions that had been caramelizing on the grill with one of those big, flat turner spatulas, and flung them straight into the gentleman's face. This caused him to cry out that he had been burned but evidently did not blind him, for the next thing I knew he'd begun stuffing pieces of so-called Texas toast into my various orifices and crevices, and though only God knows where he'd gotten that Texas toast seeing as this was not a Texas toast kind of restaurant, it really was filling me up, with toast but also with rage. Practically raving, I grabbed the gentleman by the back of the head and shoved his face into a vat of cream of mushroom soup, thinking that maybe I would just go ahead and hold it there until he drowned. Alas, he proved not such an easy mark: like a fish, he wriggled free of my grasp and at the same time managed to grab hold of the soup ladle, with which he proceeded to deliver a stinging blow to my right temple. As I staggered about from the force of it, he retrieved a large metal bowl filled with macaroni and cheese and clapped it down onto my head like a big, gooey space helmet.

Things might have gone on this way for a long time, maybe even forever, if not for the fact that, at what seemed to be the very same moment, we each noticed that our adversary was looking quite delicious in his current condition, and so, exchanging a nod of mutual understanding and assent, broke off our altercation and began eating one another. As we were every bit as delicious as we looked, we ate and ate, that gentleman and I, until nothing was left of us but these words.

The Lost Balloon

They had nine children, all of them named George except for one, who they named Georgina because from the moment she was born, one could see she would grow up to become a great beauty, and Georgina struck them as a better name than George for a great beauty.

In fact, Georgina grew up to be more of what you would call "a good-looking woman" than a great beauty, and like plenty of other people, she also grew up to be an emergency room nurse, which was how she came to meet a particular gentleman we'll call Dan.

Dan came into the emergency room one Tuesday shortly before midnight suffering from a bout of kidney stones. "Ahh!" he was screaming when he careened through the sliding glass doors. "I'm burning up inside! Save me or kill me but for the love of God, do it now!" The attending physician put him on a morphine drip and left Georgina in charge of things, and soon enough the drugs had taken their effect.

"I was really losing it there for a minute," Dan conceded.

"It's pretty typical," Georgina said. "Someone shows up screaming and hollering like that, there's basically a ninety percent chance it's kidney stones. Unless it's a woman, in which case it could be a bunch of other things, like childbirth or irrational hysteria."

"Speaking of women," said Dan, "you're a pretty good-looking woman yourself. Now that we've gotten to know each other a little bit, I was hoping to invite you to my place for a supper of pasta and seltzer water."

"Hmm," said Georgina. "I'm not sure the doctor would approve."

"It'll be our little secret," Dan winked.

Seeing as she was between boyfriends at the time anyway, Georgina accepted the invitation.

+

Dan had still not passed his kidney stone on the night of the dinner, and accordingly ate and drank sparingly.

"I'm taking a medication to relax the muscles in the bladder and prostate which will supposedly help me produce a urine flow powerful enough to blast that damn thing out of the ureter," he explained. "More to the point, I think being an appetite suppressant is one of the side effects. On top of all that, my lower abdomen and groin are in excruciating pain, which is also not very motivational as far as eating and drinking are concerned."

By contrast, Georgina could not get enough, neither of the pasta nor of the seltzer water. She ate and drank and ate and drank, and since both pasta and seltzer water cause bloating, albeit via quite different mechanisms, the more Georgina ate and drank the more bloated she became, until finally she became so bloated that she floated away like a lost balloon, drifting toward some distant star.

"Goodbye," called Dan, watching her ascend—and never saw her again.

Bob's Business

Hoping to take advantage of the stupid ass street food craze, a man known by his family and friends as an excellent enchilada chef (and also "Bob") set up a food truck downtown near the courthouse from which, every weekday during the midday hours, he offered his personal culinary specialty for sale to area functionaries. Because of the meal for which it would be eaten, he dubbed the enchiladas he sold from this food truck "lunchiladas," and had painted across the side of his food truck, just above the service window, the words "Bob's Lunchiladas."

Thanks to the fact that the downtown functionaries had just about had enough of the existing food truck options—Tibetan noodles, Nepalese fried rice, and Ethiopian beef tibs—Bob's business boomed. As the lunch hour approached, functionaries could often be heard having the following conversation across their cubicle partitions:

"What are you thinking for lunch?"

"Lunchiladas?"

"Same. Let's go together."

"Great. I'm going to ask Cindy if she wants to join us."

"Cindy, huh? Are you and Cindy, you know..."

"I'm a married man, Stanley."

"I know you are, John, but that wasn't the question."

Also, many other conversations between functionaries could be heard, all of them similar to the above in that they involved an agreement to get lunchiladas for lunch.

After some months had passed, however, Bob took a decision, the reason for this decision being that since opening Bob's

Lunchiladas he had come to adopt the entrepreneurial mindset that if you weren't constantly innovating, it was a mere matter of time before someone passed you by—one only needed to look at the aforementioned Tibetan, Nepalese, and Ethiopian food trucks, whose proprietors had fallen on hard times ever since Bob's Lunchiladas burst onto the downtown midday food truck scene, as evidence. Specifically, the decision Bob took was to start putting corn chips inside all of the lunchiladas he served from his food truck: lunchiladas that, owing to the effect those corn chips had on the auditory and tactile aspects of the experience of eating them, he re-named "crunchiladas," although inasmuch as they were still, genuinely, enchiladas that were eaten for lunch, these crunchiladas remained, at least to Bob's mind, a variety of lunchilada, rather than a fundamentally different foodstuff.

As Bob's Lunchiladas had in a relatively short time become something of a city sensation—even people who worked outside downtown were known to occasionally travel in in order to indulge in them as a special lunch treat or even, when they came in groups from the same workplace, a means of building team spirit—he was interviewed about this change by the food and wine reporter for the local newspaper. In the next morning's edition, he was quoted as having told her: "Long story short, I had a hunchilada that people would prefer to munchilada crunchiladas for their lunchiladas."

In reality, however, not everybody did. For instance, because the added crunch for which their beloved lunchiladas had been accordingly re-named left them in physical pain of a primarily facial nature, people who suffered from disorders of the temporomandibular joints preferred the original lunchiladas. But if they, or anyone else who for different reasons felt similarly, dared asked Bob to leave the corn chips out of their crunchiladas, he would begin screaming at them that without corn chips to provide the crunch, their crunchiladas would not be crunchiladas, meaning they were asking him to prepare them a logical impossibility for lunch, something only an idiot or a dipshit would do; and if, in response, they asked him for a lunchilada instead of a crunchilada, then he would really lose his temper and threaten to improve their unfortunate appearance with, as he put it, "a powerful punchilada right in the face."

Uncomfortable with all the shouting and name-calling and pugilistic scare tactics, Bob's customers began to abandon him, and soon he had no choice but to close up shop once and for all.

Reflecting on the experience in his later years, Bob would often tell people, "I guess you could say I got too high on myself and turned into something of an enchilada Nazi, but I wouldn't recommend that because then you would be making an implicit comparison between being intransigent about how you serve your enchiladas and committing genocide, and honestly the two really aren't at all comparable."

The Desires of the Dead

At a "Celebration of Life" convened on the fourth floor of a local function facility, a man clumsily embraced the daughter of the recently deceased, in the process knocking from her arms a box containing her mother's ashes, still warm from the cremation chamber. Altogether predictably, the box popped open when it hit the floor, releasing its contents into the air in a great, grey puff of the sort into which one could hardly be blamed for expecting a magician to disappear, only to momentarily reappear in the unlikeliest of locations, such as a seat at the back of the auditorium, or suspended from the ceiling like a bat.

"You twat!" cried the daughter. "I've got a half mind to slap you right across those saggy jowls of yours!"

Since it happened to be the case that the pair had once been married, she probably could have gotten away with it, too; but for some reason, perhaps because she knew from their years of marriage that the man was morbidly afraid of getting slapped and would probably scream like an owl if it actually happened, she did not follow through on the threat.

Meanwhile, pressed by a draft coming in from the stairwell, the ashes rolled across the room like some desert dust storm until, running into the wall against which a long table of food had been arranged, they gathered up and fell—mostly into a very large vat of nacho cheese sauce. Reasonably, one might expect guests at the event to have on these grounds foresworn the sauce, but in fact, nothing could be further from the truth. Put simply, they went to town on the stuff.

"It's the chips," some said, by way of explanation. "We can't let all these beautiful chips go to waste. The family must have spent a fortune on these chips!"

Others, ladling it atop heaps of ground chuck crowned with onions, peppers, and shaved lettuce, claimed they were only doing what the dead woman, herself a great lover of hot cheese products, would have wanted.

Too Much Pot Pie?

"It this a house call or are you here on business?" asked the man who came to the door.

"It's a house, isn't it?" I pointed out.

"It is," the man acknowledged, "but since I run my business out of my house, it's also a business, and there's only this one door, with the exception of the back door and the side door."

"What kind of business are you running?" I wondered.

At this point, I should mention that it would be useless to

describe the man. He was probably in his mid-fifties or early sixties, wearing saggy khaki pants, balding beneath a little nest of scraggly hair the color of steel wool, and giving off the impression that he had very itchy skin that he spent a lot of time scratching—and at that, I supposed I've just described him.

Also, I should mention that my further interrogatories revealed that he ran a lock installation and repair business. "Area Lock Installation and Repair," he specified. "I came up with the name based on the fact that I serve people in the area, although for a reasonable fee, I'm also willing to travel out of the area."

"Sounds like a pretty good racket," I observed. "You charge people to install their locks, and then you charge them again when they break."

"You don't know the half of it. With a little smooth talking, it's easy to upsell most of my customers on these fancy digital doodad electronic locks that cost five times as much as the old deadbolts and knob locks, and then when those things break, they cost five times as much to repair. I'm making a killing."

"On the other hand," I pointed out, "I'd imagine you need a lot of specialized knowledge to repair a fancy digital electronic lock, so you must have made a large investment in training on the front end."

"To the contrary, all I do is connect the fancy digital doodad electronic lock to this box that runs a diagnostic to figure out what the problem is and then runs a program to fix it. I pretty much just stand there and then when it's done, I disconnect the box and collect my fee. Actually, I collect my fee in advance, but sometimes I manage to get a gratuity out of the deal, especially from the rich old broads—pardon the expression."

"A box like that must cost a lot of money."

The man snorted. "You can get one for fifty bucks off the internet."

"Fifty bucks? Why don't your customers just buy their own?"

"Ah, but there's the rub. You have to be a certified locksmith to be able to place the order in the first place."

"Wow," I said. "That really is quite a racket."

"You still don't know the half of it," said the man. "With that little box, I can also break into my customers' houses and rob them blind. I merely plug it in, press a couple of buttons, and presto, the fancy digital doodad electronic lock opens right up. Of course, I don't take anything of significance, or they'd realize they'd been robbed and start to think the fancy digital doodad electronic lock I upsold them on didn't work so well, after all. But suffice it to say, it's been a long time, a loooooong time, a looooooooooooooong time, since I've paid for my own toilet paper."

I filled my cheeks with air and then exhaled in an effort to demonstrate how impressed I genuinely was.

"So, what do you think?" the man was saying. "Can I interest you in a fancy digital doodad electronic lock? It's the very latest in home security technology."

"Actually," I said, "I'm here about your lawn sign."

"Which one might that be?"

In fact, there was only one sign on the man's lawn—a sign the size and shape of the political signs partisans like to display during election season, but instead of ballyhooing some slime-bucket politician, it simply said: "Enough is ENOUGH." Every day I drove past it on my way to the gas station to buy enough gas to be able to drive to the gas station again the next day, and every day, I wondered what the person who'd put the sign there had had enough of.

"Today," I explained, "I decided to finally find out."

"I see." The man scratched the back of his neck, confirming my suspicion that he was itchy, and then he said: "Pot pie."

"Pot pie?" I was taken aback.

"My wife serves it every day. Breakfast, lunch, snack, dinner, and fourthmeal, should I happen to stay up late enough to require an extra repast. It's been like this for years and believe me when I tell you, I've had enough."

"Hold on right there," I said. "I've been around the block, my friend, probably about as many times as you have, and believe me when I tell you, there is simply no such thing as too much pot pie."

"From personal experience," said the man, "you can believe me when I tell you that there most definitely is such a thing as too much pot pie."

"In response to which," I responded, "I would point out that pot pie is itself a complete meal, including meat, vegetables, carbohydrates, and a mysterious gooey substance, all packaged up for the diner's convenience inside a delectable, flaky crust."

"Variety is the spice of life," the man shot back.

"A pot pie," I retorted, "is variety incarnate, with no lack of spice if it's made properly."

"Think of my health," came the man's rejoinder. "My arteries are as stuffed as teddy bears."

"You can easily rectify that situation with thirty minutes of vigorous daily exercise," I countered.

"Not with my lumbago!" the man said, raising his voice.

"Eat smaller portions!" I cried.

"I'm hungry from all my lock work and burgling!" the man shouted.

"Ask your doctor for a cholesterol lowering statin!" I hollered.

"I've tried all of them!" the man whooped. "They give me intense pain in my limbs!"

"I'm all out of arguments," I howled, "but I continue to insist that there is no such thing as too much pot pie!"

"And I that there is!" the man screamed.

"Is not!" I screamed.

"Is!" screamed he.

That was when his wife, wearing a robe and apron and coated from head to toe in flour, came hobbling into the foyer with the aid of a polished stick.

"What's going on here?" she demanded to know.

"None of your business, you old crone!" the man snapped at her.

"You'll live to regret saying that, you rusted out war-horse," the woman growled, and without a moment's hesitation began beating him with her walking stick. She beat him and beat him until he fell to the floor whimpering.

When she had retreated again into the dark part of the house, I bent down low to examine the poor fellow, and noticed that instead of blood, his wounds were leaking pot pie.

On which grounds I concluded that perhaps there is such a thing as too much pot pie.

8.
Local flavor

Poet's Tower

In the old mill town, there was a hill, and at the top of the hill—from which one could see another old mill town, nestled into a cozy little valley—there was a stone tower, and the name of that stone tower was "Poet's Tower." But was Poet's Tower called Poet's Tower because the people who went there were poets, perhaps in search of inspiration, or because, finding inspiration whether they sought it or not, whosoever went there in so doing became a poet?

A man from town who was not (yet) a poet decided to find out by climbing to the top of the hill and sitting himself down on a large rock to one side of the tower (the tower itself was all sealed up and could not be entered by anyone who did not have a key to open the padlock with which its only door had been latched) with a pen in one hand and an empty notebook open in his lap. Like that, the man waited and waited. A raven passed by overhead, landed in a nearby tree, and cawed unpleasantly—nothing to write home about, and certainly nothing to write a poem about. Then there was the view of the other old mill town, but aside from the fact that that mill town was down in the valley and this one up above it, there was nothing in particular to distinguish the two. Each, for example, was home to a thrift store, a pharmacy, a library, and two banks. Up there on the hill by the tower, meanwhile, the trees were bare, owing to the season, and everything felt very hemmed in, a geographical feature of the region that did not particularly lend itself to lyrical flourish.

"Well," said the man, at last, regarding the blank page in front of him with resignation. “I guess that settles that.”

And then it happened: a flash, if you could call it that, but one that extended itself in time, stretched out like traveling carnival taffy, just long enough for the man to write:

Poet’s Tower, O! Poet’s Tower,
This morning I forgot to shower,
And now my body odor’s sour,
But I’d rather smell like a flower,
Up here at Poet’s Tower.

The man read back over his poem once, with equal parts surprise and satisfaction. Then he gathered up his supplies and went home to take—you guessed it—a large bowel movement, a quick nap, a double dose of heart medication, and the pot roast out of the oven.

Two Adornos

The name painted in black letters on the red mailbox was Adorno; but whereas Theodor Adorno, who invented the influential philosophical procedure known as critical theory in an effort to adapt Marx's analysis of the commodity to the cultural and economic conditions of late capitalism and the so-called "culture industry," was a German-Jewish émigré who died of a heart attack in Switzerland in 1969, Gregory Adorno, who lived alone in the tumbledown house at the other end of the gravel driveway and had scrawled his name on the mailbox himself in leftover autobody paint, worked as a security guard patrolling the grounds of the nearby paper plant (which had been out of business for at least a decade, but someone still had to keep the window-breakers and other assorted mischief-makers off the property) and tossed back Buds at Jack's Red, White, and Brew on Route 5 and 10 every Friday and Saturday night. The locals, needless to say, were well-aware of the difference between their Adorno (alive) and the other (not), but from time to time some desperate doctoral student from out of town would show up at Gregory's door, greasy-haired with bloodshot eyes and a satchel of overdue library books slung over one shoulder, begging him to please, please, please help them understand critical theory before their upcoming qualifying exams.

"Honestly, I don't know a thing about it," Gregory would have to confess.

As a security guard, on the other hand, he knew quite a bit about how to wield a billy club, something several of the students who visited him subsequently discovered was at least as useful, when it came to passing their exams, as the ability to analyze the portrayal of the mechanization of leisure time and the mass production of consumer desire in Siegfried Kracauer's Georg.

But Not Forgotten

The slab of stone into which had been etched the name of the man in whose memory the elm trees were originally planted remained, but all of the elm trees had been cut down due to infection by Dutch elm disease and elm phloem necrosis, as well as for several other reasons. At one time, the stone was buried in the soil in such a fashion that its inscribed surface was flush with the grass in the shade beneath the trees in the summertime and overlaid by a latticework of shadow in the winter, but these days it leaned against the base of an electric lamppost the top of which had popped off like a mushroom cap during last night's storm and now lay shattered on the ground beside it, shards of glass and lengths of wire mingling with the snow and ice.

What could this mysterious man, this John or Edgar or David or Thomas, have done to deserve such commemoration? Perhaps, on some other chilly winter morning even longer ago, he wore shorts outside and acted like he didn't even feel cold; or perhaps, on a day when no one was expecting it, and marking no particular occasion whatsoever, he wore a whimsical hat in public without appearing to feel even the least bit bashful: a fez, with a tassel like the tail of a small horse, or a caubeen festooned with an evergreen hackle, or a top hat with a tapered crown and curled brim, encircled by a grosgrain ribbon into which had been tucked a single feather clipped from a lusty peacock's train.

Country House

In my neighborhood, from which one can catch a glimpse through the trees of a certain moderately-trafficked rural byway, there is one house that is nicer than all the others, albeit in subtle ways—for example, a low stone wall converts what for the rest of us amounts to muddy runoff into a bucolic little backyard stream of the sort beside which one seeking relaxation might sit upon a wooden chair. As it happens, the owners of this house do not even live in it; rather, they from time to time spend the weekend in it, sometimes accompanied by their children and sometimes alone, for the sake of a quick break from city life or perhaps to avail themselves of the seasonal attractions for which our area is well-known, such as the spectacle of the leaves changing color in the fall, or the annual ski jumping and chowder eating contest (two different contests, convened at the same location and on the same day, neither of which is meant to involve the use of the hands). To avoid becoming depressed by the fact that for the owners of the nicest house in the neighborhood, our community and its culture are merely an amusing diversion from "real" life, we recently decided to gather around the kitchen table to make a list of all the reasons we were nonetheless grateful to be us instead of them.

Unable to think of any, we became depressed.

9.

STORIES INVOLVING THE ELDERLY

My Old Man

Sometimes, heading into the bathroom to pee (yet again) in the middle of the night, I'll spy, out of the corner of my eye, an old man looking back at me in the mirror. "Damn it," I'll think to myself, "that old man is me," and right away start reflecting on how our lives slip through our fingers moment by passing moment, and ruminating on what I recently heard on the radio, which is that we only live about four thousand weeks on average, a statistic that can really make you question your habit of showing up at work on Monday morning wishing you could just go ahead and hit the fast forward button to Friday afternoon. Usually, it's at about this point in my thinking that I realize it's actually not me, but the old man I brought home five months ago from Fast Eddy's Old Man Sales and Service near the corner of Mill Road and Windsor Way. I bought him in the first place because I thought he'd be able to teach me how to play chess, and even though that didn't work out (honestly, it was my fault), I decided to keep him around for the occasional pearls of wisdom he imparts. Recently, however, he's started following me into the bathroom like a psychopath. "What the fuck, bro," I'll say to him, "this isn't a performance, and I sure as hell don't need an audience," to which he'll reply: "Holding a grudge is like holding a bag of shit. If it's yours, it still stinks, but for some reason the smell doesn't bother you the same as it would if it was somebody else's."

Point being, that's totally true if you stop to think about it, but I swear to God, if this dude doesn't stop following me into the bathroom, I'm going to get rid of him all the same.

The Fleece Sweater

A multi-family yard sale was convened outside a ramshackle barn not far from where I live. Having several dollars cash in my wallet, and an appetite for a good find at a good price, I decided to attend. No sooner had I arrived, however, than an elderly woman perched atop a mobility scooter on the other side of a folding table on which had been displayed for sale several old cameras and empty reliquaries undertook trying to purchase the fleece sweater I had decided to wear that morning in consideration of the weather.

"It's quite old," I informed her, speaking of the sweater.

"The best things in life always are," she replied with a wink, and what may or may not have been a lascivious grin.

In principle, there was nothing particularly fetching about this woman, who but for her rather generous proportions I would unhesitatingly have characterized as a crone. All the same, I've always been a sucker for a seductive comment accompanied by a lascivious grin, going as far back as my uneasy adolescence. I named my price and the woman accepted without delay, lumbering wheezily from her scooter and leading me into a corner of the darkened barn.

"Let's get started, shall we?" she proposed.

In preparation for the agreed-upon activities, which were admittedly deviant but as far as I know not illegal, I pulled my fleece sweater over my head, completing the operation just in time to (my eyes having by now adjusted sufficiently to the lack of light) see the flat side of a rusty shovel smashing me right in the face.

Some time later, I came to. My head ached as though I had been drinking, which I had, but I don't think that's why it ached. The fleece sweater, needless to say, was long gone, as was the elderly woman; when I stumbled squinting into the daylight, I discovered that her table had disappeared, as well, along with the various cameras and reliquaries whose weight it had sustained, and that there was furthermore no sign of her mobility scooter.

"Damn it all!" I said. "Damn it all to hell and back!"

But when I pictured her rolling down the side of some country highway with her wares strapped enterprisingly to her back and my sweater tied around her neck, flapping colorfully in the breeze, my sour mood brightened.

10.

Stories about working stiffs

Horse Inseminator

Often, I think that the only reason I keep my job, despite lacking any particular fondness for carrying out the specific duties it entails, is so that when people ask me what I do for work, I don't have to preface my response by saying, "Well, actually..." But then, on days such as today, the day before I am obligated by the terms and conditions of my employment to return to work following a long and thoroughly enjoyable vacation full of backcountry hiking and healthful foods and little hemp flower cigarettes containing only trace amounts of THC, these days also being days on which upon further reflection the idea of prefacing my response, when people ask me what I do for work, by saying, "Well, actually..." really doesn't sound so bad, I remember that the real reason I keep my job, despite lacking any particular fondness for carrying out the specific duties it entails, is that I need the money. In case you were wondering, the official title of my job, which also serves as a reasonably on-the-nose description of the duties it entails, is "Horse Inseminator." Basically, I inseminate horses, female horses, with the semen collected from male horses by, I can only hope, someone who earns a better salary than I do, and needs the money even more.

The Employee

When, thanks to a sudden departure following the settlement on terms favorable to the plaintiff of a lawsuit filed in response to a botched prostate exam, a management-level position in his firm unexpectedly opened up, a certain employee was called into a meeting with his boss and encouraged to apply.

"Geez," said the employee, who was quite modest by nature. "I'm honestly not sure I'm cut out for such an important job."

"Don't be ridiculous!" retorted his boss. "Your qualifications are rock solid, you have tons of relevant experience, and on top of all that, you've got a shitload of great ideas!"

"Okay!" said the employee. "I'll do it!"

And surely he would have if not for the fact that, heading home from work that very afternoon, he was run over by a bus.

Oh, just kidding. In fact, the employee made it home safe and sound, and soon submitted his application, completely free of typos, along with a resume he'd gone to great expense to have printed on premium quality paper with a classic linen finish.

A few weeks later, he was once more summoned to a meeting with his boss, who with tented hands and a matter-of-fact tone divulged that following careful consideration, the hiring committee had not selected him as a finalist for the position for which he had recently applied.

"We were impressed with your qualifications and experience, not to mention that super awesome paper you had your resume printed up on," he explained. "Even more, we all agreed that you had some extremely great ideas for the company. Ultimately, however, we decided we preferred someone more confident in their ability to do the job."

The employee felt disappointed, but only briefly—for as it happens, heading home from work that afternoon, he really was run over by a bus.

The Professional

Being myself a grown man, I was having an argument with a child, the particular subject of which was whether a certain artist, who the child had dismissed as merely "amateur," was in fact a professional.

"Does she make money by way of her art?" I asked the child, who had to think it over for a few moments before acknowledging that she did.

"In that case," I said, "she is, by definition, a professional artist."

The child had to think that one over for a few moments, as

well. Then she retorted: "By definition, you're professionally annoying."

Well, she was right about that much, anyway. You see, several years ago, I was hired by an eccentric billionaire to spend no fewer than forty hours per week annoying people. At first, I went about my work a bit haphazardly, sort of throwing spaghetti at the wall to see what stuck, but with the passage of time I managed to develop several reliable techniques to which I continue to entrust the faithful execution of my duties to this day. A few of those techniques include saying "chicken butt" when people ask me to guess what; tickling the palm of an individual whose hand I am shaking following a first introduction; encouraging people who have already broken and/or damaged something and/or injured themselves to "be careful"; purposely mispronouncing others' names when referring to them in the third person to their friends or relations; seizing upon the amusing stories or anecdotes people occasionally share with me in social situations as opportunities to offer unsolicited and frankly unhelpful advice; and last but not least, arguing with children.

The Promotion

An employee's performance in the position for which he had been retained was regarded highly by his superiors, and so he was promoted to a more important position—one to which corresponded a somewhat better salary.

"We're really excited about this," said his boss, who had called him into her corner office to give him the good news, and who also had a small sign on her desk that read:

Ask me about my cats

"How are your cats?" asked the employee.

"Dead," replied his boss, "but thanks for asking."

"A promotion!" he said to himself that night. "Who'd have thought?" Certainly not him. After all, he'd been perfectly happy to have acquired a job in the first place (a possibility that at one point in his life had seemed vanishingly distant), and altogether satisfied with his previous salary, which had been enough for him—unburdened as he was by a family or mortgage or even a pet—to permit himself the occasional indulgence, such as a new shirt or valet parking at the local cinema. Now, for just a moment, he allowed himself an indulgence of a different sort: closing his eyes, he imagined continuing to ascend the ranks at his place of employment, one promotion at a time, until finally reaching some position so close to the top that the place from which he had begun would appear as geometric to him, in retrospect, as a landscape regarded from an airplane. Atop the desk in his corner office, he imagined, he too would place an *Ask me about my cats* sign, and whenever some slavering underling obliged, he would reply, "Delicious," and lick a bit of froth from his chops.

Unfortunately, the employee underperformed in the position to which he had been promoted—first, there was a complaint made about him, and after that a particularly disappointing result—and consequently he was demoted to his previous position, with his salary adjusted accordingly.

"At least I know it's a position I can thrive in," he told himself by way of consolation.

But in fact, although his performance following the demotion was no worse than it had been prior to the promotion, rather than regarding it highly his superiors now regarded it with suspicion, and soon enough the poor fellow found himself out of a job.

11.
More stories about husbands and wives, and also food and death

A Man, His Wife, a Fox, a Fly

A man was in a lot of pain.

"Maybe it's all in your head," said his wife.

Which was actually true, inasmuch as the specific source of his pain was a headache.

Therein was about to end a short and simple story, but just before it could a fox, wandering past the window above the author's desk, wandered into it and bit the poor man right in the scrotum. And why did the fox bite that poor man in the scrotum? Because that poor man's scrotum happened to resemble a fuzzy little mouse, and everyone knows foxes love to prey upon fuzzy little mice.

"Ow!" shouted the man, by the way. "My scrotum!"

The good news was that getting bit in the scrotum by a fox had caused him to completely forget about his headache as a result of something called task-related analgesia, although technically speaking, getting bit in the scrotum by a fox probably doesn't qualify as "a task."

At about this juncture, the author, thinking he could do no worse, decided to stop writing for the day and head for—it really doesn't matter where, but let's just say it was most definitely not, yet again, the local discount appliances store—and en route it occurred to him that the fly that had been buzzing around the inside of his car for the past three days was probably wondering what it had done to deserve all this applause.

Clap, clap, clap, went the author, removing both hands from the steering wheel, at which point the car, left to its own devices, veered into the path of an oncoming truck, and in such a manner this story—but not the fly—finally did meet its end.

The Man Who Took Leave of His Wife

The man took leave of his wife, who was busy rolling large balls of lint into an even larger ball of lint from which she would, come wintertime, pull handfuls of lint to use as tinder in the fireplace, and then he set out on his way. Having driven several miles, he realized he'd forgotten his checkbook, which in consideration of the specific nature of his destination he was likely to need, and so he was obligated to return home.

"Oh, it's you," his wife remarked, looking up from a bowl of dough she was in the process of punching with what appeared to be great vengeance, when he walked into the kitchen still wearing his driving shoes.

"I forgot this," he said on his way back through, holding up his checkbook and wagging it.

"Oh," she said. "That."

Once more, the man set out on his way, but having once more driven several miles, he realized he'd forgotten his wallet, which one needs regardless of the specific nature of one's destination—for instance, in case one is pulled over by the police who, if one does not have one's wallet and is therefore "driving without a license," may throw one in the slammer, where one may be subjected to harassment and even physical violence or unwanted romantic advances. For this reason, the man was once more obligated to return home. Passing through the kitchen, he offered no explanation to his red-faced, perspiring, dough-punching wife, but on the return trip he held the wallet aloft, much as he had the checkbook, and wagged it in her direction.

"You'd forget your own head if it wasn't attached to your body," she snorted, and gave the dough a wallop.

Now, this man was a patient man if nothing else, but when it came to adding insult to injury, that was simply more than he could abide. Without so much as exchanging his driving shoes for his yard shoes, he stomped through the high grass behind the house to the storage shed to retrieve his angle grinder, with which, back in the kitchen, he proceeded to saw off his head in order to subsequently direct toward his wife a dramatic performance of not forgetting it despite the fact that it was plainly no longer attached to his body.

"And now?" she asked.

"And now," said the man, holding the freshly sawed-off head by its (thinner than he'd realized) hair, "I take my leave."

"Again?" asked his wife.

"Again," the man confirmed.

In consideration of the upholstery, he wrapped the head with newspaper from the recycling bin before placing it gently atop the passenger seat of the car, and at that, he was on his way. As far as he knew, he had not forgotten anything else this time around, apart from where he was going and how to get there, but disaster soon ensued all the same: unable to see a thing, he plowed first through a crowd of activists who had gathered on a nearby street corner to protest the rising cost of grain, and then straight into a gas station, provoking a powerful detonation in which many people, including the activists and the man himself, were killed.

"All I can say is I hope it was worth it," his wife said to him at his funeral.

But the man did not say a word.

How She Got to Florida

After initiating a fiber supplement, a man began shitting like crazy. He shitted and shitted.

"I'm a shitting machine," he informed his wife of several decades.

"Blessings and felicitations," she replied.

"Actually, it's getting to be a little much," the man told her. "I don't have time to do anything else. My golf game, for instance, is in shambles."

"Maybe you should stop eating for a while," his wife suggested. "After all, what goes in must come out, so I'd assume the opposite is also true."

"That's just the thing," the man said. "I haven't eaten a morsel since I believe last Wednesday, if I'm not mistaken."

"Nothing?"

"Water and air," said the man. "And supplemental fiber, of course."

His wife, who was not strong when it came to mathematics, used her fingers to count the days that had elapsed. "Hmm," she said, then. "In that case, whatever you're shitting out definitely can't be food."

"That's what's got me worried."

"Hey," the man's wife replied. "What really matters is that you're shitting again, am I right?"

"I guess," said the man.

But come morning, the man was dead.

In order that he might be subjected to the proper procedures in terms of disinfection and embalming, his wife—who was now his widow—brought him to the nearest mortuary, only to find herself being turned away at the door.

"I work with bodies," explained the mortician. "What you have here is an empty bag."

"What kind of bag?" inquired the widow.

The mortician shrugged. "That depends on what you put inside of it, I suppose."

So, in the spring she used it for transporting her parafoil kite to and from the breezy field near the lakeshore where she liked to take it soul flying to the rhythms of the music in her head; in the summer, she brought it to the farmer's market and stuffed it to the gills with fresh produce, blocks of hand-milled soap, and tins of artisanal beeswax lip balm; in the fall, she filled it with dead leaves from the yard, which she later emptied into a great and rancid dead leaf pile at the town dump; and when winter came, she packed it up with a bathing suit and enough clothes to last until the spring and headed down to Florida, where a Spanish sailor on shore leave taught her how to say "¡Ay, caramba!" all night long.

Dread

Splish-splash: a man was enjoying his morning urination.

"Help!" he suddenly cried out. "I'm dying!"

"Not to worry," said his wife from the adjoining bedroom. "Remember, we ate beets for dinner last night."

"It's not that," the man explained. "It's that out of the blue, it just occurred to me that since death is the natural and inevitable terminus of life, the fact that I'm currently living means, paradoxical though it may seem, that I'm also currently dying."

"Oh, pshaw," said his wife. "You've got to change your thinking is all. For example, instead of telling yourself you're going to die, tell yourself that the whole concept of death is really just something we humans have invented in order to be able to put a name to that which resides beyond the limits of our capacity for imagining the future."

"So you're saying I'm not going to die?"

"I'm saying that the first law of thermodynamics is that the total amount of energy in the universe is a fixed quantity. How did Einstein put it—nothing dies, it just changes form. But if your very capacity for imagination is part of your present form, how could it possibly extend itself to whatever form or forms the energy from which that present form is constituted will assume next?"

"I guess that makes me feel a little better," the man said.

That was when he noticed the blood-red swill swirling in the toilet bowl beneath him.

"Help!" he cried out. "I'm dying!"

All the Coffee in the World

As he was preparing his coffee for the following morning, a man noticed that the inside of his coffee maker was filthy with old grinds and other detritus. Leaning forward to have a closer look, he whacked his head on the corner of an overhanging cabinet. After that, all the coffee in the world couldn't wake him up.

Well, that's what the doctors, the coroners, and the biologists said—but his wife, desperate, determined that the theory that in sufficient quantity, coffee couldn't wake a good man from the dead, had not actually been put to the test, and that, lacking any better options, she was going to be the one to finally do it. For days, she poured coffee into the gullet of her late husband's corpse. Much of it simply spilled back out onto the shirt he had been wearing at the time of his demise, but some of it dribbled down his esophagus.

"You should give up," suggested her friends.

"This man has died," announced the doctors.

"This man has been pronounced dead," declared the coroner.

"Reanimation of the dead is both theoretically and practically impossible, regardless of what those scam artists who offer to keep our bodies on ice until such time as we have figured out how to bring ourselves back to life might claim," explained the biologists.

But the woman, relentless, went on dumping coffee into the dead man's gullet, undeterred by the increasingly pungent odor of his corpse.

Then, one day, right in the middle of this dumping, the corpse's eyes fluttered open.

"It's a miracle!" the woman cried.

The no longer dead man's tongue flicked out of his mouth, and he licked his lips the way one does after awakening from a deep sleep. Then he said: "If it's not too much of a bother, would it be possible to switch to a French roast?"

"A French roast," repeated the woman.

"If it's not too much of a bother," repeated the man.

The woman was nonplussed; her husband, as she had known him in life, would never have asked for a French roast, which the two of them agreed from the time of their first meeting was a variety of coffee only people who didn't know anything about coffee thought was good coffee, but that in reality tasted like campfire ashes and barbecue sauce. What's more, she would have never married a French roast drinker in the first place. Imagine that awful, smoky smell first thing every morning! Yet, the fact that her husband was alive again and apparently a French roast devotee, meant that, having not divorced him during his death, she was now, in spite of her best efforts, married to a French roast drinker.

"There's only one thing to do," the woman said under her breath.

"What's that?"

"Oh, nothing. I was just saying how glad I was to see you alive again. Now let me go get that French roast you were asking for."

Her husband relaxed on the sofa while she traveled across town to a grocery store in a neighborhood populated by people with no taste, where she bought a tin of the cheapest, most disgusting French roast they had in stock.

"Perfect," her husband said when she showed it to him. "Just what I had in mind."

She suggested that, as she was not much of a French roast drinker herself, he prepare it to his own liking.

“Good idea,” he said. “I need to get up and get my blood flowing, anyway. Right now, everything’s still a little—tingly, I suppose is the word.”

But as he was preparing this French roast, the recently resurrected man noticed that the inside of his coffee maker was filthy with old grinds and other detritus and, leaning forward to get a closer look, whacked his head on the corner of an overhanging cabinet.

After confirming that he was deceased once again, the woman called the funeral parlor of her choice and arranged to have the cadaver retrieved.

“I don’t suppose I could bother you for a cup of coffee before I hit the road,” the body retrieval technician they sent for the purpose asked once he’d attended to the business at hand. “It’s been a heck of a day and I’ve got long drive ahead of me.”

“French roast?” the woman asked.

“God forbid,” replied the technician.

A week later, they were married. To celebrate the happy occasion, friends and family of the new couple pooled their resources to buy them the best self-cleaning coffeemaker on the market.

Avocado Toast Cabaret

For lunch, the man had prepared himself a slice of avocado toast.

"How very modern of you," observed his wife, arching her eyebrows.

"What did you want me to have?" asked the man, resenting the implication. "Pot roast? Stewed rabbit? Mutton? It's a healthy lunch, and if they happen to eat it in Hollywood so be it. I'm not going to deny myself just because I'm afraid someone will accuse me of being a what do you call it?"

"A poser," said his wife.

The man proceeded to sprinkle sunflower seeds atop his avocado toast.

"Sunflower seeds," observed his wife.

"What?" said the man. "They're a superfood. Okay, fine. I don't know if they're technically a superfood, but they're packed with fiber and other nutrients, which is pretty super in my opinion."

Next, he shook some hot pepper flakes atop the sunflower seeds.

"Hot pepper flakes," observed his wife.

"I like a little spice," the man said. "You could say that in my case, spice is the spice of life."

"Since when?" asked his wife.

"Since recently," said the man. "I'm in a state of constant evolution, and it's good thing, because if you're not evolving, then what's the point?"

"What's the point of what?"

“Of just—of anything. You name it, there’s no point to it if you’re not evolving.”

It occurred to the man that a cool beverage would both complement and counteract the spicy flavor of the pepper flakes. With this in mind, he removed a glass from the cupboard, intending to fill it with a refreshing combination of sparkling water and low-calorie lemonade sweetened with Stevia, a natural alternative to sugar; a moment later, a second glass, which must have been somehow held in place by the first, tumbled out and shattered against the countertop, spraying shards of itself this way and that.

“Ay, caramba!” the man said. “Chimichanga! Carlos Berlanga!”

“Who?”

“Oh, no one,” the man explained. “Just an important Spanish cultural figure from the 1980s.”

“Ah,” said his wife. “The famous Movida Madrileña. A true cultural florescence.”

The man swept the glass up off the floor and wiped down the counter. Then he carried his piece of avocado toast to the table—it was on a plate, I should mention—and sat down in front of it, licking his chops like a dog at the bone.

“Wait a second,” said his wife. “Don’t tell me you’re going to eat that.”

“Of course I am,” said the man. “It’s my lunch, remember? That thing you eat in the middle of the day, somewhere in between breakfast and dinner.”

“What about the glass?” asked his wife.

“What about it?”

“Don’t you think some of it ended up on your toast?”

The man cocked his head. “I don’t see any.”

“That’s probably because it’s mixed in with the avocado and

all that other pretentious crap you put on there."

"Well even if that's true," said the man, "I'm extremely disinclined to throw away a piece of avocado toast. Have you seen the price of avocados recently? Not to mention the price of bread, which is your basic substrate of toast, if that's the right word. And sunflower seeds and hot pepper flakes are no bargain, either. Between supply chain bottlenecks and the price of diesel gasoline, commodities are through the roof all around, which you would know if you listened to Marketplace on National Public Radio every afternoon the way I occasionally do. Even more importantly, what's it to me if I eat a little glass? Back in the days of traveling carnivals, there was always someone in the sideshow whose job was to eat light bulbs, and the last I checked those people weren't going around choking to death on their own blood like Atilla the Hun."

"What the hell do you know about traveling carnival side-shows?" asked the man's wife, crossing her right leg over her middle leg and her left leg over her right.

"A hell of a lot more than you do," the man said, grasping his toast between the hooked fingers of one of his claw-shaped hands.

"I'm not so sure about that," said his wife, stroking her long, corn-silk beard.

"Let's ask him what he thinks," said the man, in reference to his conjoined twin.

The Bum

"You've always been a good-for-nothing, and this proves it," his wife, who was endlessly berating him, berated him when he announced that, having had just about enough of it all and then some, he'd be becoming a bum and moving into a leaky old tent down by the river.

Disinclined to give her the satisfaction of being right yet again, he formulated a plan: instead of just becoming any old bum, he'd become the best bum. Or, in any event, a very excellent bum. A good enough bum, anyhow, that it would no longer be possible for her to say he wasn't good at anything, because he'd have clearly demonstrated that he was good at being a bum, his having become which would therefore turn out in the long run to have disproven the very thing she was so certain it had proven.

Of course, since no matter how you cut it, being a bum is a form of being bad at things—at life, generally speaking, and then also at more specific things, like earning money or securing a place of residence—it was also the case that one could only be good at being a bum by being bad at being a bum; and since "good" and "bad" are relative terms, insofar as, for example, as very good youth baseball player would probably be a very bad professional baseball player and so forth, if he was going to be good at being a bum, i.e. bad at being a bum, he was in fact going to have to figure out how to be even worse at being a bum than the majority of the other bums.

Luckily, it wasn't difficult for the man to find a solution, which was that at dinnertime, when the other bums would open their cans of beans with rusty old can openers or edgeless pocketknives, he would just beat his against a rock until it split and then scoop the contents directly into his mouth using his bare hands.

"I'm impressed," conceded his wife, who had come down to the river to berate him for old time's sake. "You really are bad at this."

The New Husband

The holidays being upon him, a man walked into the sort of shop that's tended to by a clerk in a little black beanie.

"I need a gift for a good woman," the man declared. "Anything in this pop stand of yours fit the bill?"

"Hmm," said the clerk from underneath his little black beanie. "I suppose that depends on what exactly you mean by good."

"Oh, you know," said the man. "Stays in shape. Does the

wash. Cleans up after most of my bad habits…"

"In that case, might I recommend a new husband?"

The man thought it over. "On the one hand," he said, finally, "that could put me out of business, in a certain regard. On the other, I do see the appeal."

"Let me show you what we have in stock."

The clerk took him to the new husbands section of the shop, just in between the Japanese bathmats section and the marijuana-scented candles made from soy section.

"I've got one of these," he said, pulling a new husband off the shelf. "And I've also got this guy in a couple of different sizes. And this fellow here has generated a lot of buzz on the internet—I'm surprised he hasn't sold out yet."

"Jesus, Harold, and Christ," said the man, checking the price tag on one that had captured his fancy. "I'm a machinist, my friend. I make a respectable salary when it comes to buying the bacon and the eggs, but something like this is beyond my financial possibilities."

"I'll tell you what," offered the clerk. "I do happen to have one of last season's models in the storeroom that I'd be willing to let you take off my hands at a fifty percent discount, if you'd have any interest in something like that."

"Could be I would. What color is he?"

"Don't you know you're not supposed to describe what color another person is anymore?" replied the clerk. "It's like saying what kind of food a fat person looks like. Used to be okay, now it's considered insulting."

"In that case, just bring him out and I'll draw my own conclusions."

The clerk obliged.

"I'm liking what I'm seeing," said the man.

+

That evening, after dinner and a couple of drinks, the man presented his wife with her holiday gift.

"Oh, jeez," she said. "I don't know if I can handle having to deal with two of these things. Do you think I could exchange him for store credit."

"Pleasure to make your acquaintance, ma'am," said the new husband.

"On second thought," said the wife, "he's perfect."

"Great!" said her old husband. "Where should we put him? I was the thinking over the fireplace. I could take my long gun down and mount him in its place. Or if you're not into that, there's always that chair nobody sits in."

"Seeing as he's kind of a replacement you," the man's wife said, "it seems to me what would make the most sense would be to put him in your spot in the bed."

"My spot in the—? Where the hell would I sleep?"

"You could sleep right on top of him."

"I'd end up with a crick in my neck!"

"How about the couch?"

"You already know I'd throw my back out!"

"Sorry, but unless you can think of something else, it's going to have to be one or the other."

As throwing his back out was a less appealing prospect, all things considered, than getting a crick in his neck, the man opted for former.

"You okay under there?" he asked the new husband when he settled his weight on top of him. "I know I've let the years accumulate on me, as they say."

"Hrmmrrrllgbblrgrr," said the new husband.

"Sounded like a yes to me," said the man.

But when he returned from the bathroom early the next morning, tugging a pinch of underwear fabric from between his buttocks, he found his wife sitting upright, pointing at her new husband.

"What did you do to him?" she was saying. "He's blue!"

"Hey, hey," said the man. "Don't you know you're not supposed to describe what color another person is anymore. It's like saying what kind of food a fat person looks like. It's considered insulting."

"Well I don't think we need to worry about insulting this guy," replied his wife, "because in addition to being blue, he's also dead."

"Dead?"

"Dead. You asphyxiated him with all that blubber of yours."

"Let's see here." The man gave the new husband—who was, in fact, looking quite blue—a few slaps in the face. "How about that? He is dead."

"Goddamn it," said his wife. "Now what are we supposed to do?"

"You know I can't think on an empty stomach."

"Same."

For breakfast, they had bacon and eggs.

Then, they dragged the new husband's corpse down to the basement and tossed it into a box with all the other useless gifts they'd exchanged over the years.

12.

Two Insane asylum stories

How I Ended up Insane

Owing to a rather dramatic cabinetry issue, I was visited by a carpenter who, while I prosecuted unrelated matters, undertook to resolve it. At a given moment, the carpenter interrupted me in my prosecution of the aforementioned matters, informing me that while the job was, for all intents and purposes, complete, with respect to a couple of finishing touches he realized that he had left an important tool in his nearby carpentry studio, for which he was accordingly departing.

"I'll be back in fifteen minutes," he pledged, and tipped his carpenter's cap at me deferentially.

Yet, fifteen minutes passed, and still the carpenter was not back. And then fifteen more. To make a long story short, the carpenter never came back because on the way to his nearby carpentry studio, he had been violently run down by a car.

As you have probably deduced by now, the driver of the car by which he was run down was me. To put it simply, I didn't give two shits about the carpenter's so-called "finishing touches"—the job was, in his own words, for all intents and purposes already complete, and this was more than good enough for a lifelong bachelor such as myself, who has no use for the domestic flourish. Consequently, I ran the carpenter down in order to be able to gain the advantage of his labor without having to pay for it, inasmuch as dead carpenters don't send bills.

Some might say that to run him down the way I did, in broad daylight in the middle of a busy intersection in front of countless eyewitnesses, was insane. Those people would be correct, but likely overlooking the fact that it was intentionally so: once I'd decided on my course of action, I quickly determined that one way or another I was eventually going to be found out, and that it would therefore be most advisable to conduct it in an insane fashion so that, taken before a jury of my peers, I would be able to plead not guilty by virtue of insanity of the crime of which I would stand accused, and then point to the very crime itself as proof.

The jury was every bit as easily bamboozled as I'd anticipated, but not so, it seems, the staff at the otherwise agreeable insane asylum to which I was, their verdict once pronounced, dispatched posthaste by the presiding judge; for upon my arrival—I know not whether as a form of vengeance sought on behalf of the carpenter, who admittedly did nothing to deserve his fate, or merely because they did not want a sane person enjoying the privileges of their facility—they immediately set about trying drive me insane. The main way they did this was to deny that I had ever run down any carpenter. For example, if I began describing to my fellow residents the crunch of the carpenter's bones, like gravel beneath the wheels of my car, the next thing I knew an orderly would be patting me gently on the shoulder saying, "There, there, you never even owned a car," while at the same time another would be wrapping me up from behind in a restraining implement and holding me firm while the first plunged a syringe into my buttocks, and the next thing I knew after that I'd be waking up in my little room with the lights on and the door locked from the inside, drenched in an ice-cold sweat. And then there was the time a carpenter was brought inside the facility to address a problem with one of the benches in the sauna and he looked so much like the carpenter I ran down that I could only assume they'd gone so far as to retain the services of an unscrupulous professional makeup artist for the purpose of confusing me.

Sensing an opportunity to put an end once and for all to their constant tomfoolery and skulduggery, I leapt upon the man, intending to extract the truth from him in a public forum, if necessary by force; but as usual, the orderlies were at the ready with their restraining implements and syringes.

"The sauna?" they laughed when, once revived, I complained to them bitterly about the incident. "You don't really think we'd give you loony tunes a sauna, do you? Get a load of this guy over here talking about a sauna!"

And who could forget the food? One day, they served kangaroo, which made me so jumpy I could hardly sleep; the next, bear, and I could hardly bear it.

The Man with a Lot to Do

A man with a lot to do woke up one morning worried he wouldn't be able to get it all done.

"I've got a lot to do," he said to his wife, "and I'm worried I won't be able to get it all done."

"And I don't have jack shit to do," yawned his wife, "so I'd appreciate it if you'd respect my freedom to keep sleeping by zipping up that big piehole of yours."

On that note, the man went to the kitchen to make himself a cup of coffee. The coffee, as it turns out, was delicious—rich yet crisp—but its deliciousness did not prevent him from continuing to worry that he wouldn't be able to get all the things done that he needed to get done. And then what? When would these things get done, and by whom? And if they didn't get done...?

Not knowing where else to turn, he decided to put in a call to his friend the early riser.

"I've got a lot to do," he explained, "and I'm worried I won't be able to get it all done."

"What I lack in charisma," replied his friend, "I make up for with my lack of charisma."

"Okay."

"Alternate version. What I lack in charisma, I make up for with my charming lack of charisma. Which do you like better?"

"The first," said the man.

"Why?"

"Because you have to give your audience a little rope, if that's the right expression."

"It's not."

"You get the idea. Besides, what does this have to do with my problem?"

"Nothing," said his friend. "It's just that I've been working on some new material and your, shall we say, unexpected call seemed like a propitious opportunity to try it out. Take it for a test drive, so to speak. Kick the ol' tires."

"Are you some kind of stand-up comedian now or something?"

"That depends on how much quality material I'm able to come up with. You want to hear another one?"

"Sure."

"Okay. You know how when you're wearing cut-off shorts in the summertime, there's always some wise acre who comes along and says, *hey, someone stole half your pants?*"

"I guess."

"So, my idea is when that happens, I say, *to the contrary, someone returned half my legs.*"

"Ha ha," the man said. "That's pretty funny, actually. Although at the same time, from a practicality perspective in terms of actually doing stand-up comedy, it wouldn't work unless you were first of all wearing cut-offs, which could be problematic because a lot of clubs have a dress code for the purpose of discouraging unruly behavior, and second of all, even if you were wearing cut-offs, you'd still need someone in the audience to actually say that thing that you said, which honestly seems pretty hit or miss."

"Yeah, well who fucking asked you, anyway?"

"I thought you were looking for feedback!"

"Only if it's positive."

"Fair enough. Now what about my problem?"

"Listen," said the man's friend. "I'm no certified life coach with a specialty in actionable deliverables, but the one thing I'd say is that no matter what, you absolutely cannot let this situation drive you insane."

"Why not?"

"Just trust me, okay. I've got a cousin."

"Everyone's got a cousin."

"Not like this cousin. He once threw a computer monitor out a second story window."

"And?"

"And it fucking broke, what do you think?"

Persuaded, the man immediately turned his attention to the task of not letting the situation drive him insane.

Unfortunately, his efforts were unsuccessful, which is how he found himself watching TV in the lounge at the local insane asylum exactly one year later when his friend the early riser's debut stand-up comedy special came on the air.

"Hey," the man said, pointing. "I know that guy."

"Sure you do," sneered the orderly, and slapped him hard in the back of the head.

13.

WARNING: The following stories are INAPPROPRIATE

The Turtle

The man, in the interest of general fitness and robust longevity, was out for a jog despite the weather, when his need to defecate, in and of itself hardly surprising considering the circumstances, took on an unprecedented urgency. Luckily, he was not far from his home, to which he returned forthwith, repairing directly to the bathroom.

After several minutes, he emerged.

"That was a close call," he reported to his wife, who was in the living room making various calculations. "By the time I got here, the proverbial turtle's head was already poking out of its gluteal shell."

Immediately, his wife filed for divorce, a process the completion of which required a visit to the local judge.

"She's claiming irreconcilable differences," the judge explained to the man. "Do you have any objections?"

"Yes," said the man. "The truth is, what's behind all of this is nothing more than the fact that, with respect to an urgent need to defecate that I had recently experienced while jogging, I told her that by the time I got home the proverbial turtle's head was already poking out of its gluteal shell."

Upon hearing this, the judge sent the man straight to jail, where he was assigned to share a cell with a brawny fellow who after days of ominous silence divulged that he was in for Capital Murder and various other Class A felonies, including battery with a battery.

"What about you?" he then asked the man.

"Basically," the man explained, "what it all comes down to is that I was out for a jog and almost shat my pants, but luckily I made it back home just in time, and after doing what I needed to do in the appropriate location, I came out into the living room and told my wife, well my ex-wife, that by the time I got home the proverbial turtle's head was already poking out of its gluteal shell."

Emitting a great and terrible roar, the man's brawny cellmate grabbed him by his hair, dunked him face-first into the fetid water festering in the bowl of the metal toilet that was pretty much sitting right out there in the open on one side of the cell and furthermore did not have a lid, and flushed it without delay.

"Gurgle, gurgle," said the man.

Following this incident, the man was directed by the team of guards that soon arrived on the scene to gather up the small number of possessions he'd been allowed to bring with him to jail—a toothbrush, a couple of pornographic magazines, and a magnifying glass—and prepare to be relocated, for the sake of his own safety, to a single-occupant cell.

"It's not your fault," one of the guards escorting him to his new cell said as they walked. "He's a very violent person."

"I guess," said the man. "But honestly, everything between us was pretty much fine until I told him about how I told my former wife, in reference to an urgent need to defecate that I had recently experienced while jogging, that by the time I got home the proverbial turtle's head was already poking out of its gluteal shell."

In a flash, the guards set to bludgeoning him with their cudgels. Then they threw him into solitary confinement. For weeks, he sat in a windowless room so small he could not even stand or stretch out his legs to sleep. Periodically food was passed through a narrow slot that opened for this purpose in the otherwise solid metal door, but since the food was always the same—flavorless and of an indeterminate texture—it gave him no information about what time of day or night it might have been.

Soon the solitude and sensory deprivation drove the man so insane that he began conversing, as one does, with the walls.

"What's it like being walls?" he asked them.

"You know," the walls replied with a shrug. "I mean, what you see is pretty much what you get. I wouldn't say it's boring but, well—it's a job. Would I do it for free? Technically, I guess I am currently doing it for free, so yes. But seeing as I'm literally a wall, I'm not really sure what else I'd do besides be a wall. I mean, advertising would be my first choice in terms of an industry I've always been able to see myself working in, but by the same token, you don't see a lot of walls working in advertising."

"Hey," said the man. "Believe it or not, I worked in advertising before all this crap started. Well, marketing. Telemarketing, I should say, but the point is, I had a good life. Man—if only I could go back in time and never tell my then wife, in reference to the urgent need to defecate I'd just experienced while jogging, that by the time I got home the proverbial turtle's head was poking out of its gluteal shell."

Momentarily, the walls began to shake with such fury that soon enough they crumbled, giving the man a perfect opportunity to escape his confinement. Sirens whooped and strobe lights swept back and forth across the great open fields behind the prison, but the man ran and ran until he reached a bog or possibly a swamp into which, having nowhere else to go but back where he'd come from, he plunged. Then, step by painstaking step, he began to slog upstream, in what he hoped would turn out to have been the direction of Canada.

Hours later, worn out from so much slogging and in need of a rest, he spotted a rock on the muddy banks of the swamp or bog.

"That looks like a fine pillow," he said. "Then again, if you're tired enough, anything's a fine pillow."

He climbed out of the muck and lay down, settling his head upon it.

"Hey!" said the rock, scuttling out from underneath him.

"Holy shit!" said the man. "A talking rock!"

"I'm not a rock, you idiot," said the rock. "I'm a turtle."

"Now that's a coincidence," replied the man.

"Oh yeah?" said the turtle. "How so?"

"Well, I almost hate to tell you this, but the whole reason I'm in this mess is that, describing an urgent need to defecate that I had just experienced while jogging, I told my now ex-wife that by the time I got home, the proverbial turtle's head was already poking out of its gluteal shell."

"Why would you hate to tell me that?".

"Oh, you know. I suppose because, being a turtle, you might feel like I was implicitly comparing your head to a piece of my poo."

"No, no," said the turtle. "I'm a real turtle, whereas what you were talking about was a proverbial turtle. There's a big difference. Big."

"That's very reasonable of you," the man said. "If only people were that reasonable—well, no need to dwell on the what ifs, is there?"

"Listen," the turtle said. "It doesn't take a Sherlock Holmes to deduce that you've been having a bit of a rough go of things recently, so how about I give you a little blowjob to calm your nerves?"

"A blowjob?"

"Did I stutter."

"From a turtle?"

"I'll let you in on a little secret, my friend. Turtles give amazing blowjobs, mostly owing to the fact that we have no teeth but very muscular tongues."

“Gee,” said the man said. “I mean, on the one hand, I could definitely go for an amazing blowjob—and that does sound like it would make for an amazing blowjob. But on the other hand, I don’t even know whether you’re a dude or a chick.”

“Having established that I’m a turtle, does my gender presentation really make a difference?”

The man was forced to concede that, all things considered, it did not.

“So, what’s it going to be?” the turtle asked. “I might be a slut, but I’m not slutty enough to wait around all day for you to make up your mind.”

“Fuck it,” said the man “Why not?”

“Great!” said the turtle. “You won’t regret it!”

But the man did regret it, because no sooner had he taken his dick out than that backstabbing bottom-feeder bit it right off.

Two Nurses

Two nurses were doing that thing nurses sometimes do where they sit behind a long desk and pretend not to hear the patients crying out for help. I should also mention that these two nurses were both women, had worked together for a long time, and knew each other's families, which is what makes it okay that when one of them yawned, the other said to her: "You know that every time you yawn a ghost sticks its dick in your mouth."

"Is that so?" asked the nurse who had yawned.

"So I've been told," replied the nurse who had not.

"Ha ha," said the first nurse. "My poor dog, in that case."

"Help me!" cried out a patient from somewhere down the hall. "My bed is on fire!"

"Ha ha," said the second nurse to the first, both of them pretending not to have heard the screaming patient. "My poor cat, you mean. Cats yawn way more than dogs!"

That was when the ghost breezed in.

"Cat schmat," he said, arriving with a blustery whoosh. "Did you ever stop to think about me, racing all over the globe sticking my dick in people's mouths non-stop without so much as a lunch break? I mean, thank God for time zones because I don't see how I'd manage it if everybody in the world got that two-thirty feeling at the same time. But on the other hand, it's also all because of time zones that when it's bedtime on one side of the planet, people are just waking up on the other, and here I am bouncing back and forth between the two like a ping-pong ball, doing my best to get my dick in and out of every yawning mouth before it snaps shut. Anyone who thinks Santa Claus has it tough ought to spend a day in my shoes."

That was when Santa Claus came trundling in.

"Oh, fuck you and your miserable little dick," he snarled at the ghost through his pillowy beard. "I should slap the living shit out of you right now."

"Whoa there," said the ghost. "I'm not trying to talk down on your work, which is one hundred percent a major part of the global economy with respect to, for example, variable costs, not to mention amortization and lagging indicators. By the same token, if you stop to do the math, there are obviously a lot more yawns per day than there are Christian households with chimneys, and that's leaving aside the obvious, which is that you only have to perform your amazing feat of circumnavigation once a year, whereas I literally haven't had a day off since I died."

"Yeah, yeah, yeah," said Santa. "You're probably right. I guess I'm just a little sensitive when it comes to people complaining about their dicks on account of that I lost my own to frostbite decades ago."

"Oh, wow," said the ghost. "As in you lost functionality, or as in you lost the actual dick?"

"Picture a mushroom without its cap," Santa elaborated.

"Oh, wow," said the ghost. "That really sucks, man. I honestly can't even imagine. And my sympathies to Mrs. Claus, as well, by the way."

Santa let out a disdainful snort. "Mrs. Claus, my ass. The last time that dusty old bitch opened her legs, a flock of pantry moths came fluttering out."

"Ha ha," said the ghost. "Ha ha ha. You may have lost your dick, Santa, but you sure haven't lost your sense of humor. I'll tell you what. How about I buy you a drink to make up for this little misunderstanding of ours?"

"Make it two and you've got yourself a deal."

"Two it is," declared the ghost, and arm-in-arm, the pair headed for the elevators.

Meanwhile, from somewhere down the hall, a patient was screaming: "Help! Somebody, please help! I'm completely engulfed in flames!"

Bisexual Porker

Upon splitting from her husband and subsequently expanding her dating pool to include both men and women, a theretofore slender woman decided that her greatest desire in life was to slap people and for it feel to them like getting hit in the face with a package of hot dogs. However, since even relatively small hot dogs were much larger than her fingers at the time this decision was taken, the woman knew she would have to gain a great deal of weight in order to reach her goal—so much that some of it would have nowhere else to go but to her furthest extremities.

To accomplish this feat, the woman began eating substantial quantities of many different things. Some days, she ate up to a half-dozen extra-large Beef Stuft Burritos from Taco Bell, each of which contains a whopping 870 calories and 41 grams of fat, the majority of them derived from partially hydrogenated oils. Other days, she focused on guzzling cola and pounding boxes of Honey Smacks, considered by leading experts in the field the least healthy cereal available for purchase on the open market. And then, of course, there were the days dedicated to birthday cake and hunks of chocolate fudge the size of cinder blocks.

After various months had passed in this manner, the woman one morning looked down at her fingers and thought to herself, they are finally as big as hot dogs. To put her theory to the test, she slid the forefinger of her left hand into a hot dog bun and squirted a squiggly line of ketchup on top of it and, beside this squiggly line of ketchup, a squiggly line of mustard. Yes, indeed: were the finger not attached to her hand (and her hand to her wrist, etc.), she could as easily have sold it at the local baseball stadium, and no one would have thought twice before giving it a hearty chomp.

At once, the woman commenced trying to slap whosoever came within reach. Unfortunately, owing to her newfound corpulence she now moved so slowly that everyone she targeted easily dodged the blow and then, while she huffed and puffed from the tremendous effort that had been required for her to lift and swing her great war hammer of an arm, chuckled and said: "Better luck next time, you bisexual porker."

Discouraged, yet disinclined to let all those months of gorging herself go so easily to waste, the woman decided to take out a classified ad in the city's weekly alternative newspaper offering readers the opportunity to, as she put it, "willingly suffer being slapped across the chops by a bisexual porker with fingers the size of hot dogs in exchange for fifty dollars cash." Response to this ad was so overwhelming the woman initially feared she'd go broke; but thanks to a widespread misunderstanding with respect to what was being paid for, and by whom, she ended up becoming quite wealthy instead.

The Well-Endowed Madman

He was a very wealthy gentleman who had made his fortune selling grain, or perhaps lithium batteries. More recently, he had spent most of that fortune funding a nationwide campaign to raise awareness of the fact that, as he himself put it on the thousands of billboards he paid to have erected along highways and byways from coast to coast, and the millions of pamphlets he paid to have distributed in various YMCAs and town halls and sports arenas and airport waiting areas and fast food restaurants, "size really does matter"—not just when it comes to movie monsters and casino jackpots, as we were all already aware, but also when it comes to actual human penises.

The reason he had become persuaded that size really does matter when it comes to penises, and accordingly inspired to invest so heavily in persuading others of the same, had nothing to do with questions of what we might call sexual prowess: after all, this gentleman knew as well as anyone that it is not the size of the boat but the motion of the ocean. Rather, he had learned that from time to time, during the ever more frequent periods of intense heat and extreme cold by which our ailing planet is plagued, rats living in sewer systems beneath the towns and cities and endless rural outposts with which we have populated it have been known seek relief from the conditions by swimming upwards through the network of drainage pipes that evacuate into those sewers until reaching some toilet by way of which to access (even if the seat is closed, most sewer rats are more than muscular enough to lift it) the comforts of a temperature-controlled human residence. Additionally, the gentleman had learned that, though rare, it is by no means unheard of for one of these rats to make its way into a toilet in the foregoing manner at the very same moment that someone is seated upon it. On the basis of these facts, the gentleman concluded that, permitted by its owner to dangle between the legs in what might be called the "traditional" style, an extremely or even merely very long penis would, whether because mistaken for foodstuff or confronted as a stalactitic obstacle, in such a situation find itself at risk of being bitten by the surfacing rat, at which point the best case scenario for the victim would be a painful physical healing process and perhaps even more painful process of emotional healing, and the worst a bout of gangrene eventually leading to amputation of the afflicted appendage.

As for the money he invested in the awareness-raising campaign, the gentleman fully expected to make it all back and then some by, once having sufficiently spread the word, manufacturing and marketing a special garter-like device that could be used to fasten a penis to its owner's thigh for the duration of his or her sojourn on the toilet, thereby maintaining it at a safe distance from the jaws of any surfacing rats. Unfortunately, he was unable to see these entrepreneurial plans to fruition; in a desperate bid to hold on to the scant remains of what once promised to be a quite handsome inheritance, his shiftless son successfully petitioned to have him committed to the local loony bin, where—his predecessor having recently been released after unexpectedly going sane—he was promptly introduced to me as my new roommate.

"What're you in for?" I asked him on our first night together, and he told me. From the fact that I have since died of terminal constipation, reader, you are welcome to draw your own conclusions.

The Writer and the Shitter

A writer running dangerously low on ideas for the silly little stories he liked to write was shitting in a public restroom one day. As it happened, this writer had a particular policy when it came to shitting in public restrooms, which was that even if he had finished shitting, he would not leave the stall in which he was shitting unless or until the restroom was empty—it had something to do with the fact that, though he had no problem with talking about shitting in the abstract, he was altogether uncomfortable with anyone but members of his immediate family knowing, concretely, that he had been shitting, no less when and where.

Well, on this particular occasion, another gentleman entered the restroom, settled into the stall beside the stall in which the writer was shitting, and also began shitting. This other gentleman had hardly begun shitting when the writer finished shitting, but per his policy the writer was obliged to wait him out. As a result, he was there when, rather than flushing the toilet and being on his way after he had finished his shit, the gentleman in the stall beside him instead stood up, turned around, and took a giant piss right on top of it.

Now here, thought the writer, was something to write about. He had never imagined anyone doing such a thing, no less witnessed it firsthand. But—he couldn't help but wonder, several hours later, as he looked back over his completed work—was the wider public toward a certain chimeric idea of which all of his literary labors were ultimately directed really going to be interested in a story about a gentleman shitting in a public restroom and then standing up and taking a huge piss right on top of it?

In short, FUCK YES! No sooner had this story been published than readers began to flock to it, and critics to fawn over it. Within a week of its release on Amazon.com, it received a perfect five-star rating from over 30,000 verified purchasers. College professors who hastily added it to their syllabi reported enthusiasm such as they'd never seen from students who usually sat at their desks glassy-eyed or playing video games on their mobile phones, or sometimes a bit of pocket pool. Film rights to the story were even optioned by a major Hollywood production studio, which only backed off actually producing a cinematic version on account of the unprofitable NC-17 rating it surely would have received from the Motion Picture Association of America. With respect to the aforementioned critics, we might highlight as exemplary one, in particular, who (though he was later revealed to have been suffering from a condition owing to which he thought he was still living in the 1990s) described it, in none other than the prestigious New York Times newspaper, as "Precisely the kind of story we need to see us through difficult times such as these."

Unfortunately, the spectacular popularity of the story ensured it would soon make its way back to the gentleman about whom it had been written. As it turned out, he was something of a private sort of fellow himself, and though his personal anonymity had been scrupulously maintained (after all, not even the writer himself was aware of his identity), he was displeased, highly displeased, to see the details of his bathroom habits widely disseminated in this manner. Revenge, he vowed upon reaching the end of the story (despite his displeasure, it was so riveting he couldn't help but finish it), would be his.

There are, of course, many ways for one seeking vengeance to attain it, but the method preferred by this gentleman was to place a smudge pot under the hood of the offending party's car and wait patiently for it to have its effect. Hence, our writer can currently be found standing by the side of the road in the middle of winter watching his beloved 2009 Toyota Prius go up in flames.

And whether he'll write a silly little story about the experience remains to be seen.

Versions of These Stories Have Previously Appeared In

"Idea"—*Nunum*
"Go To Hell, Kevin"—*Apocalypse Confidential*
"The Boarder (Three Deaths)"—*Expat Press*
"Pain"—*Expat Press*
"The Snack"—*Bullshit Lit*
"A Most Literal Town"—*Overheard*
"Story with a Joke"—*BarBar*
"Fran, Who Became a Crow"—*The Corvus Review*
"Two Pregnancies"—*Neon Garden*
"The Ice Skater"—*Maudlin House*
"The Lovelorn Leg"—*Sublunary Review*
"The Man Who Was Considering Soaking His Own Beans"
—*The Dribble Drabble Review*

"Too Much Cheese"—*Bullshit Lit*
"A Passion for Pork"—*Berfrois*
"Rest Stop"—*Berfrois*
"The Lost Balloon"—*A Thin Slice of Anxiety*
"Too Much Pot Pie"—*Johnny America*
"Poet's Tower"—*The Argonaut*
"Two Adornos"—*Ghost City Review*
"But Not Forgotten"—*Rejection Letters*
"My Old Man"—*Ligeia*
"Horse Inseminator"—*Johnny America*
"The Professional"—*Maudlin House*
"A Man, His Wife, a Fox, a Fly"—*Bullshit Lit*
"The Man Who Took Leave of His Wife"—*Misery Tourism*
"Dread"—*Berfrois*
"Avocado Toast Cabaret"—*A Thin Slice of Anxiety*
"The Bum"—*Bullshit Lit*
"The Man with a Lot to Do"—*Berfrois*
"The Turtle"—*The Bear Greek Gazette*
"Bisexual Porker"—*The Squawk Back*

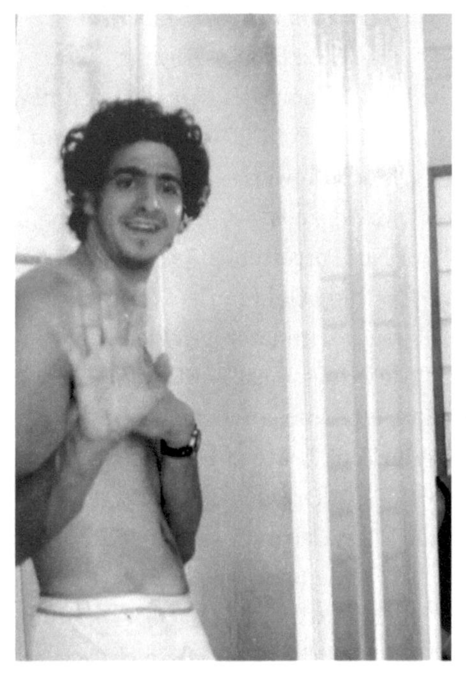

The author in his male modeling days

www.ingramcontent.com/pod-product-compliance
Lightning Source LLC
Chambersburg PA
CBHW021753190726
48290CB00008B/2600

* 9 7 8 1 7 3 4 8 9 3 0 2 1 *